HELL'S BELLS

(Welcome to Hell #6)

Eve Langlais

Edited by Devin Govaere
Copy Edited by Amanda L. Pederick
Line Edited Brieanna Robertson
Produced in Canada

Published by Eve Langlais
1606 Main Street
PO Box 151
Stittsville, ON
Canada
K2S1A3
www.EveLanglais.com

ISBN-13: 978-1530077984
ISBN-10: 1530077982

Chapter One

@GaiaLuc4ever: Hiding in the garden. This is not a game. HE is on the loose. #evilspellssuck

"I KNOW YOU'RE HIDING," he sang. The melodic taunt echoed all around her. "There you go, playing games again. But I will find you. I *always* find you."

The scary yodel invaded the sanctity of her garden, and Gaia couldn't help but tremble. *Please don't let him find me.*

She hunched lower in the hopes of blending into the foliage. She held her breath, closed her eyes, and prayed—to herself. *Go, go, earth magic.*

The garden, with its chlorophyllic sense of humor, thought it funny to betray her. Branches rustled as they parted.

"There you are!" The exuberant exclamation had her prying one eye open. She almost lost it at the brightness of his Hawaiian shirt. "I found you, my darling snookums. Such a playful girl you are." Lucifer wagged a finger at her. Wagged it while smiling.

Wrong. So wrong—sob—and she couldn't handle it anymore. She'd reached the point she would have given anything—even the rights to some lumber crews to mow down a few forests mortal side—for a scowl from Lucifer. Some sign that the evil overlord she'd fallen in love with still resided somewhere inside that delicious body.

And she did mean *delicious*. Not just to eat, though, even if she did enjoy doing that too. Standing a few inches over six feet, with perfectly cut dark hair, a chiseled physique, and deep, dark eyes to make her swoon, her lover and fiancé had shed all the glamor spells hiding his true self. No longer did he hide his grandeur behind a mask, a mask he lost when Ursula cursed him with being nice.

Ugh. The horror of it. Who wanted a nice guy? Certainly not Gaia. Part of her reason for loving the big, bad demon was his totally alpha a-hole personality. But that bold and outspoken demon was gone, replaced with this candy-assed polite idiot who didn't even attempt to raspberry her breasts, even though she wore her best push-up bra.

That's just wrong! My girls need attention. I need attention. There had to be a way to fix her demon lover.

She'd already tried slapping and screaming at Lucifer. He'd just turned the other cheek!

Since when did the Lord of Sin forgive?

She tried seduction, splaying herself in lingerie upon his massive bed. He showed her respect and offered to sleep in the guest bedroom.

Attempts to just plain ignore him resulted in him bringing her candy and potted plants.

Potted. Plants.

Not cut from-the-vine or stem blooms. This new polite version of Lucifer refused to kill plants.

What a wuss. And he was all hers. Could she get a resounding ugh?

"Let me help you up." He offered her a gentlemanly hand to stand from the bushes she crouched in. With a heavy sigh, she took it, and he hauled her to her feet with a strength he kept restrained. The old Lucifer would have yanked her off balance and made sure she fell against his hard body. Then groped her.

This one set her politely aside—without a single indiscreet touch—and asked, "How is my darling snuggle muffin today?"

"Thinking of jabbing sharp sticks in my ears." So she didn't have to listen to the syrupy nonsense spewing from his mouth.

"Why do something so painful when, instead, you can partake of culinary delights? You must have forgotten, my sweet cupcake. We have the cake tasting today. A perfect wedding isn't complete without the perfect cake." The bright shine of his teeth in the stretched grin held a hint of madness.

At least she thought so. Lucifer's face wasn't made for pleasant grins. Smoldering looks, scowls and wicked intention, yes! Sweet and inviting? No. Just no. It was so utterly wrong.

"Can't we just get your palace chefs to whip something together?"

He clasped his chest—a wasted move since Lucifer didn't have a heart. Hadn't in ages, having hidden it a long time ago. "Perish the thought. I want nothing but the best for my pumpkin-spiced latte delight on her special day. A day that is getting close. Just think, my delicate flower, soon we'll be together. Forever."

Cue the ominous music. Why did he have to remind her? Bad enough she didn't know how to get through the next hour with the torture he promised. She refused to imagine a lifetime with this candy ass.

Luc, oh Luc, where are you? Not in this body, that was for sure. "I don't want to taste any cakes. I hate cake." She preferred flaky pastries with whipped cream and fresh fruit.

"Hate cake? How is that possible?" he said with dramatic flair and not a hint of sarcasm. "I love cake. It's my absolute favorite, especially when smothered in buttercream icing." He licked his lips and rubbed his belly.

How sad his declaration made her, sad because, until the ill-fated engagement party, his favorite dessert had been pie, her pie to be exact, which he claimed tasted like cinnamon and apples.

How Gaia missed the way Lucifer ate her pie. The new Mr. Manners hadn't touched her since their party, claiming he was saving himself for their wedding night. Here she dated the biggest manwhore in all of Hell, and she couldn't get any action. Meanwhile, she was out of fresh and firm cucumbers.

Don't judge. Organic was all the craze these days, plus she was allergic to most rubbers and latex.

"Shall we, my darling?" Lucifer gestured grandly at the portal he called, a swirling mass of colors, a new addition since he claimed the dreary black version of before lacked invitation.

She let loose another heavy sigh as she let him grasp her hand. "Coming, Luc." And not in a way that would cause earthquakes and tsunamis.

#thinkingoftryingazucchini

Chapter Two

@GaiaLuc4ever: 5 days until I get to see my beautiful bride walk down the aisle. #soexcited #squeeeeeee

ODD HOW NO ONE LIKED his newest status update. But Lucifer couldn't worry about that now, not when something awful drew all his attention.

Gaia had lost her smile. Something ailed his precious lady. Utterly unheard of and unacceptable.

Give her some sausage. That will make her smile, or gag. Either way her mouth will have something to do.

Lucifer ignored the crude thought. He was having such trouble with that nagging voice in his head. It kept trying to escape the pretty cage he'd put it in, and when it did manage to slip out, it suggested the vilest things.

It is not vile to want to taste some pie. Or throw that sweet piece of ass over our shoulder and have our wicked way.

Such actions were improper for a couple unwed.

Exactly. Which is why it's such damned good sex.

No sex until their wedding night. And they'd do it for the right reasons. To procreate.

Spoilsport.

Since the voice seemed irritable, again, Lucifer gave it a warm mental hug. The gesture sent the voice—which, for some reason, he couldn't help picturing as a horned rubber duckie—recoiling and quieted the discontented murmurs for the moment.

Good thing because Lucifer couldn't afford the distraction, not when he needed to figure out the flower arrangements for the wedding. He'd encountered such a dilemma with that, given the bouquet he planned was limited by flowers he could arrange to receive in silk. Nothing would mar his precious lady's day, especially not the murder of her plants.

"What do you think?" he asked, holding up a finely wrought bunch of pale, delicately petaled roses. "Do we go classic arrangement? Or…" He held up another bunch of blooms, a vivid medley of colors. "Do we make sure we cover as many flower genres possible so none of her garden is offended?"

His youngest daughter, Muriel, blinked at Lucifer, but didn't reply. He worried about her hearing. He worried about a lot of things where his youngest was concerned, such as the fact that she was unwed and had a child out of wedlock. Various discussions, though, about repairing her personal life always seemed to upset her so much.

"Have you thought about legalizing your commitment to your gentlemen friends to something a little more permanent?"

"They live with me. How much more permanent can it get?" Muriel asked.

"Your child deserves the legality of marriage, not to mention marriage is a beautiful commitment to the person or, in your case, persons, you love."

"Who are you, and what did you do with my father?"

He patted her hand as he said, "Don't try and divert the subject. I understand this is difficult for you, and I want you to know"—he stared deep into his daughter's eyes—"I'm here for you."

"I wish you weren't. I miss my real daddy," she sobbed.

The old daddy she referred to had lived a sinful life Lucifer refused to dwell on—even if his voice kept trying to remind.

He locked those naughty, naughty memories away and strove to be the demon he should be. A demon who needed to pick out flowers.

"Well?" He shook the bundles at Muriel. "What do you think? Single bloom or many?" Again, she blinked and didn't say anything.

Poor girl was probably overcome with emotion, given her mommy and daddy were finally going to tie the knot and make her legitimate. He still didn't understand how he'd allowed this travesty to go on for so long.

Don't worry, baby girl, Daddy is going to take your bastard stigma away.

You say bastard like it's wrong, moaned his inner duckie.

"I think," Bambi said, drawing Lucifer's attention, "that you should let Gaia choose."

A rare frown knit his brow at his oldest daughter's suggestion. "I planned to, and yet when I asked Gaia, she burst into tears. Poor love muffin. She's so overwhelmed with all the preparation involved for our big day. I'm just doing my best to take some of the pressure off her. I love her so much." So much he just had to hug himself tightly, wishing he squished his Gaia right now in his arms.

Yeah, hold her close. Naked. Those soft curves begging for—

Door slam. Mind out of the gutter. He needed to respect Gaia.

Muriel made a choking sound and fell forward, banging her head off thc desktop.

"Sweet baby girl," he exclaimed as he dropped his flowers and rushed to her side. "Are you ill? Do you need Daddy to call you a doctor?"

"No," she sobbed against the smooth bone surface of his old desk.

"Want Daddy to kiss your booboo better?"

"No!" Muriel wailed louder.

His eldest daughter, who wore an entirely too short skirt and clingy blouse instead of the loose slacks and blouse he'd bought her, drew him away from the desk. "Little lamb over there will be fine. She just is feeling a little overwhelmed with all the details requiring her attention to run Hell."

"And what a wonderful daughter she is for taking over so I can concentrate on my upcoming nuptials with her mother." Muriel banged her head again, making him wonder if she needed a hug. "I do so appreciate all her hard work."

"I wish you'd tell me to fuck off and stop trying to steal your job. Maybe even send an assassin or two after me," Muriel muttered, lifting her head to peer at him with eyes that burned with the fires of Hell. "Or how about making me gag by dragging mother into a corner somewhere, in plain sight, and trying to seduce her?"

"I would never defile your mother!"

"Yet I really wish you fucking would. Defile her until she screams and you strut around bragging about how you're the demon."

"Language, my sweet daughter!" Lucifer exclaimed. "You are much too pretty to spew that kind of vulgarity."

"Fuck. You." Muriel enunciated very clearly, punctuating her misbehavior with a raised middle finger.

"Young lady, I am a tolerant demon, but you have pushed me too far. You know very well that kind of behavior is not allowed." He pointed off to his left, hating to pull the stern-parent routine, but loving his daughter too much to allow her down the path of sin and disrespect. "March yourself to your room until you can comport yourself in a manner befitting a poised princess of Hell."

"I'll behave when Hell freezes over." She scowled. "Again. Goddammit!"

"And don't take my brother's name in vain," he added as his daughter stomped out of sight. He shook his head and tsked as he returned his attention to Bambi. "I don't know what's gotten into her. She seems so different since the engagement party."

"Are you sure she's the one who's changed?" Bambi asked, peeking at him from under a hank of blonde hair.

Arms went flying into the air as Lucifer gesticulated. "Why does everyone keep asking that? You all act as if I'm the one who's suddenly switched his personality overnight. Yet, I've never felt better."

"You're wearing pink pastel slacks and a Hawaiian shirt with pineapples."

"I know. Utterly amazing." He peeked down at his ensemble. "I know it's a sin to have pride, but it's a bigger sin to lie and say that I don't look dashing."

"I miss your penguin suspenders and your evil shark tie."

The reminder of the items in his wardrobe that he'd had to dispose of embarrassed him. "No fear, daughter. I've rid myself of those silly fashion choices."

No, not the duckie slicker! the voice in his head yelled.

He threw a warm, fuzzy blanket of love over the cage to quiet it.

"Have you been to see Nefertiti?" Bambi asked.

"Why would I see the venerable sorceress? There is nothing wrong with me."

Such a lie, snapped his insidious friend.

Yes, he told a lie, a white one, which made it totally acceptable.

You are not fine. For one thing, you hear voices.

He did, and yet Lucifer saw no need to worry anyone with the fact that he seemed to have an itsy bitsy split-personality issue. Things were under control.

Bambi perched on the tabletop strewn with silk flowers. Her short skirt rode up, and he wished he could find a large blanket to cover her with.

"I think you should see her," Bambi insisted. "Nefertiti has some other tests she'd like to run."

With an indifference he didn't have to feign, Lucifer waved a hand. "I adore you for your concern, daughter. But I'm fine. Now, tell me what you think." He whipped the bouquets into the air again. "And keep in mind, I am getting the bridesmaids' dresses to match."

How about we shove those flowers where the sun doesn't shine? growled his caged other half.

How about another hug?

Argh.

#ilovehugs

Chapter Three

@GaiaLuc4ever: Meet me in the garden for a plan of attack. We need the Dark Lord back. Pronto. #teamevillucifer

BANG.

The buzz of conversation died as Gaia slapped her hands down on the tabletop and drew all eyes to her. Quite a few people had gathered around the solid wooden table that rose from the garden soil, the bark smooth to the touch, and warm too. In her special garden, trees weren't murdered for paltry reasons like furniture. But when she did require the niceties of society, her plants loved to give a helping frond.

"Thank you all for coming," she began, only to find herself immediately interrupted.

"Oh no. Not more freaking manners," Muriel grumbled aloud. "Bad enough I've got Dad being all courteous and polite. Don't you start too."

"I'm with the princess. If I hear the words please and thank you from the Dark Lord one more time, I might go on a murderous rampage," Psycho Katie announced.

"Like that's anything new," Xaphan stated in a low tone that nevertheless carried. "Or did you not notice the pile of bodies this morning in the coffee shop?"

A wicked grin lit Katie's features. "Totally

justifiable homicide. The barista put two pumps of cocoa in my java when I specifically asked for three."

"Grounds for rampaging," someone muttered.

"Totally agree," piped in another.

"We should firebomb head office."

The agreement came from just about everyone there. They were minions of Hell after all. Sin was a virtue they all coveted, but not the point of this meeting.

Bang. "Shut up and listen!" Gaia dropped the niceties. Muriel had a point. Everyone in Hell was sick of saying their please and thank-yous, and the culprit behind that was the reason they were all here. "As you are all aware by now, Lucifer isn't quite himself."

"If by not himself you mean a freaking prat," griped Niall. "Never thought I'd say I preferred him better as a prick."

"We all preferred him as a prick," Gaia agreed. *Some of us preferring his prick more than others.* "But obviously there is something majorly wrong with him since Ursula gave him that blasted kiss of peace." A kiss she should have never allowed. Gaia's fault for not succumbing to a jealous rage. It wouldn't happen again. *Next time any woman tries to lock lips with my man, I will ensure they're pushing up daisies.* Her little blooms did so thrive on decomposing flesh.

"I still can't believe my magic didn't cure him." Muriel pouted. Her poor daughter had made an attempt to drive the curse on her father out. She brought a new man into her harem for extra mojo then went on a sexual escapade that blasted a wave of insanely powerful magic meant to erase all spells. It worked ridiculously well, wiping the glamor on Lucifer that made him seem older, erasing all the spells, new and old, layering his body. But it didn't take care of the curse plaguing him most. The curse of niceness.

Nefertiti, currently in her nubile form and shape of an Egyptian beauty, drummed long, lacquered nails on the table. "As I keep mentioning, none of my scrying has managed to find any curse or spell on the Dark Lord."

"So it's buried deep," Ysabel, his longest enduring secretary, stated. "Keep looking. It's got to be there somewhere."

"It would help if the Lord of Sin would return to my laboratory for more tests." Nefertiti pinned an accusing gaze on Gaia.

She raised hands in a don't-blame-me gesture. "I've tried. He insists there's nothing wrong with him and that your skills would better serve the public. For free."

Dark eyes flashed as Nefertiti spat, "Philanthropic blasphemy. Magic should always have a price."

"And warning labels," Marigold piped in as she twirled a fluorescent green strand of hair. For every concoction Marigold managed to produce correctly, three others went sideways—and, in one case, had escaped into Hell's sewers.

"If it's not magic, what else could it be?"

"Body snatchers." The odd suggestion came from Jenny.

Gaia blinked at her. "Are you suggesting aliens took over his body?"

A red hue invaded Jenny's cheeks. "Not quite. I guess I should explain. See, Felipe made me watch some mortal realm movies. Body Snatchers was one of them. It got me thinking. What about if, when Ursula kissed the devil, she passed on some kind of parasite? Something that wasn't magic-based but organic, which is why nobody can detect it."

The suggestion, while met with a few raised brows, had merit.

"You know, I never even thought to check for a bug, but still, my initial scans should have shown something."

"Unless it was an alien microbe," repeated Jenny. "Seeing as how Ursula escaped her banishment to another dimension, maybe she returned contaminated."

"It's possible she brought something through with her." Nefertiti tapped her chin as she mused aloud.

"I'd say more than probable. I mean just look at SWEETS and the other monsters inhabiting the new Wildling ocean. It's not farfetched at all to conjecture the Dark Lord is infected with something from another dimension, given it's nothing we've ever seen before," Adexios said. The fellow sat at ease on a polished rock about chair height. Boney knees—he took after his father, Charon—peeked through the worn holes in his jeans, and his T-shirt stated he hearted *Star Wars*. Behind him, Valaska, dressed in leather straps and not much else, stood at attention, ready to kill anything that might attack. Amazons did so love a good fight. They were also known to start some if bored.

No fighting in her garden. Gaia kept strict control on who was allowed into her secret garden, and she also governed what happened in it. Anything that might crush her delicate plants under clumsy warrior feet was strictly prohibited.

"Sweets?" Katie frowned at Adexios. "You have alien candy and didn't share? I feel a murderous rage coming on."

Xaphan slapped an arm in front of her before Katie could launch herself. "Relax. He means SWEETS, as in his pet sea monster."

"It stands for She-who-eats-exquisitely-tasty-screamers," Muriel's new beau, Tristan, added. "My father is quite jealous of Adexios. The alien sea monsters he's encountered have all ended up as dinner instead of pets. Dad is most put out."

And probably tugging his beard. The man did own a lavish one, usually braided with seashells, for he was Neptune, god of the sea. Although more recently, folks referred to him as the disgruntled ex-husband now that Ursula had returned to Hell. Neptune now fought a never-ending battle to keep control of the Darkling Sea. However, the new Wilding Sea kept encroaching onto his territory.

"We are getting off topic," Muriel reminded. "Daddy would be so proud. I mean, would have been." Lucifer's daughter burst into noisy tears. "I want my daddy back!"

David patted her on the back while Auric shrugged. "She's been doing that a lot since she took over as interim Dark Lord."

It wasn't easy taking on the sins of the world. Gaia's daughter tried since Gaia's lazy stepson, the antichrist, refused to. But Muriel was feeling the effects.

"Let's return to the idea of a parasite," Gaia said to bring the focus back on the problem. "How would we go about testing for it?"

"Full body exam," Nefertiti suggested. "Bring

him to my lab."

"Any ideas on how to get him there willingly?" Gaia asked with a grimace.

"Use your feminine wiles. Shake those tatas." Katie winked as she rolled her shoulders.

"Tell him you baked some cookies and get him to follow. Always works for my wife when I work too much," Charon suggested, his voice floating from within the cowl of his robe. The man had the mystery aura down to a science.

In the end, she went with Ysabel's suggestion. "Since the Dark Lord no longer believes in violence, then I say we jump him. Chances are he won't fight back and we can drag him to the crone's lab."

"That's evil crone," Nefertiti snapped.

"Whatever."

It took a few more arguments, name-calling, and a fistfight Gaia quickly broke up before they were in a wicked enough mood to go jump the former Dark Lord.

He helped matters when he looked up from the book he was reading—featuring a rainbow on the cover—and said, "I am so happy to see all of you. Group hug!"

They hugged Lucifer all right and dragged him, politely complaining all the way, to the deepest, darkest bowels of the castle.

He didn't once try to set them on fire.

Never even tried to have them confined to hard labor and lashes.

Lucifer did worse than that; he forgave them.

#needsastiffdrink

Chapter Four

@GaiaLuc4ever: 4 days until I show all of Hell my great love for Gaia. #loveherwithallmyheart

THE CARING ALL HIS friends and family displayed when abducting him for an examination made Lucifer forgive their rather violent methods. He knew he didn't require medical attention, but they were so concerned about him that they ambushed him, bound him tightly in enchanted chains, and carried him to the dungeon lab, which he noted was in major need of a cleaning and some white paint.

As he lay on the stone altar, with the carved channels meant to carry fluids away and the iron bolts embedded in thick concrete through which they looped his chains, he smiled at everyone who cared so deeply for him. "I'm fine. Just fine. I appreciate the concern, and I can't wait to hug you all when you set me free."

His daughter turned away with a cough, her shoulders shaking, overcome with emotion.

Lucifer's most stoic warrior shook his head. "I say we put a plastic bag over his head and put him out of his misery," muttered Xaphan. "The Lord I knew wouldn't want to live this way."

Fingers snapped as Nefertiti swept into the room. "Before we resort to permanent measures, why don't we see what's going on? Scissors please."

Nefertiti held out her hand, and someone slapped the tool into it.

Upon her first snip of fabric, Lucifer couldn't help but screech. "Stop! Please don't cut my clothes."

The sorceress's dark eyes fixed him. "We need to remove your garments that we might better examine you."

"It's the 'we' part I'm not comfortable with. You're talking about denuding me in front of a crowd." He lowered his voice. "A man shouldn't show off his naked parts to the ladies. It isn't proper." A man his age should practice modesty.

"But everyone's seen your junk," Katie remarked. "There are dozens of sex shops in the merchant ring that have modeled their vibrator collection after it."

Lucifer could have died of embarrassment as his keen employee reminded him of the follies of his youth. "I am so ashamed of my previous exhibitionist actions. Modesty is the righteous path."

"No! Just no. I can't take this anymore!" Remy pushed through the crowded people, anxious to leave the lab.

The poor demon was overcome with emotion as Lucifer expressed remorse.

More like horrified. He knows it's a crime to hide our virile manhood from the ladies.

Nonsense, Remy left because he understood Lucifer's need. "If you insist on conducting this examination, then might I ask for some privacy?"

At his request, silence filled the room, broken only by the sizzle of the burning torch.

"Did he just say…" someone whispered at the back.

"Yes, he did."

"Someone should check for snow. Again."

Oh yay, more of the fluffy stuff. Funny how so many of his recent actions were, for some reason, being tied to the snowflake and ice events.

"You heard Lucifer. He wants privacy, so everyone out," Gaia ordered.

Lucifer could tell by the tears in his beloved's eyes that she appreciated him showing such modesty. As Lucifer's future intended, she didn't want any other ladies getting a peek. He wondered if she would politely avert her gaze. Hopefully she wouldn't look. It would make their wedding night so much more special. He couldn't wait to join with Gaia.

It's called fucking, you freaking repressed moron.

No, it was lovemaking because Lucifer would be merging himself body and soul with the woman he loved.

You are sucking the joy out of everything, moaned his inner voice. *We should have let Xaphan kill us. I should jump into the abyss.*

Suicide is a sin, Lucifer reminded his other self.

Exactly.

Fingers snapped in front of his eyes.

"Luc? Luc? Are you in there?" Gaia peered at him with evident concern.

"Right here, my beloved flower."

She cringed. "Everyone is gone from the room except for me and Nefertiti. She is going to cut off your clothes now."

A shame. He rather liked the outfit he sported today. The bright yellow slacks and the button-down, collared shirt really brought a hint of sunshine to this place.

The air this far down in the castle proved a touch chilly, and he shivered as the fabric parted and peeled back. To keep himself warm, he kept his gaze on Gaia, who paced at the foot of the medical altar.

How beautiful she appeared with her hair pinned atop her head in a messy cascade. Today she sported a lovely frock that shimmered in the candlelight and clung to her womanly curves.

Such beautiful, luscious curves.

Remember touching that smooth skin? How she likes to cry out when our lips leave scorching kisses as we make our way down to her neatly trimmed forest…

Lucifer did remember. But he shouldn't. Fornication out of wedlock was a sin. A big sin.

He forced himself to look away, yet that didn't stop the memories from staining his mind.

The image of her cheeks flushed, her mouth open, her back arched…

The feel of her fingers digging into his back…

No. No. Stop it. The sinful reminders warmed his body, especially a certain part.

Naked, he couldn't hope to hide it, and his erection did not go unnoticed.

"I see at least one part of him is working fine," snickered the sorceress.

"Now there's a surprise," muttered Gaia. "Given he hasn't touched me since the engagement party. I was beginning to wonder if Ursula's kiss had rendered him impotent."

Gack. Argh. Ugh.

The voice in his head went in paroxysms. Apparently, it took great insult in Gaia's words. Lucifer saw only the care and concern.

"Nothing ails me," he reassured her.

It didn't erase the line of concern on her forehead. "Okay, Neffie. Where should we begin the examination?"

Nefertiti began at his feet, which made him giggle. Her small and deft hands palpated every inch of him, except his manparts, while his inner voice chanted, *"Touch it. Touch it. Touch it."*

"Please don't touch me in my private place," Lucifer begged.

"You don't want her to touch you?" Gaia asked, her brows arched high.

Why the surprise? She knew his feelings on intimacy.

"It wouldn't be proper for her to touch me"—he lowered his voice—"there."

"I see." Gaia tossed the remnants of his shirt over his genitals. "Let's leave that part alone for now."

"If you insist." Nefertiti skipped over his penis—giggle—and continued up his body.

Snort. I can't believe you think of it as the P word.

Of course Lucifer knew the correct word for it. But it wasn't something one should say blithely aloud.

You're right. The P word should never be used. Cock. Dick. Rod of pleasure. Now those are words.

La-la-la-la-la. He hummed to avoid the litany of crude names for men's parts.

Nefertiti shone a light in his eyes, a magical beam that shot from the tip of her finger. She peered into each of his ears. Made him open his mouth and say "Aaaah." Even parted the follicles of his hair and checked his scalp.

"I can't see a bloody thing out of place," she grumbled. "All of his parts seem intact, the right size, and in fine working order."

"No!" Gaia practically wailed the word and then threw herself against him. He would have dearly loved to hug her and pat her back to tell her everything was fine, but all he could manage was, "It's a good thing she didn't find anything. Don't cry, keeper of my heart."

Gaia raised her head, and he noted her eyes shone bright with tears. "What did you call me?"

"Keeper of my heart." He smiled.

She did not return it. Instead, she moved away from him and dragged Nefertiti to a corner. They whispered, but he didn't eavesdrop. It wasn't polite.

When they returned, Nefertiti conjured a stethoscope out of mid-air. Placing the listening buds in her ears, she then leaned over to place a cold metal probe against his chest.

"I'll be fucked by my harem times two," she muttered. "I didn't have a clue it was there. The Dark Lord has a heart."

"No he doesn't," Gaia stated. "At least he's not supposed to."

"Of course I have a heart, silly billy," Lucifer stated with a laugh. "I have a great big one, and it's full of love for you!" He beamed.

Gaia walked out.

Probably to work on her vows. The wedding was getting close after all.

More like she left to sharpen a stake.

I love you.

Fuck off!

#allweneedislove

Chapter Five

@GaiaLuc4ever: Found out my fiancé has a heart. #someonegetmeastake

STALKING FROM THE medieval chamber, Gaia tried to come to grips with the revelation that Lucifer had a living, beating heart in his chest.

Impossible.

He couldn't have a heart, and not just because the lord of the pit was supposed to be a heartless bastard. He didn't have one because he'd hidden it millennia ago. She knew this for a fact. Heck, she didn't have one either and for the same reasons as Lucifer.

One, no one was truly immortal. Everyone sported a certain Achilles heel.

The damned ones, the souls that came to Hell upon death on the mortal plane, had the Pit. The abyss at the center of the nine circles of Hell acted as a recycler for souls. Damned one jumped in, and somewhere, a baby born got a new, clean soul.

Demons could die by numerous means in Hell—but in a strange twist those same wounds on the mortal realm just sent them back to the nine circles for shaming by their brethren.

The Lord of Sin was practically invincible, except for one fragile thing. His heart. Decapitate Lucifer while he wore it in his body and the Dark Lord could perish—if the person knew to incinerate it in the furnace that warmed Hell. Knowing this weakness, Lucifer had removed that pesky organ from his chest a long time ago and hidden it. Not too many people knew that secret.

Gaia did.

She also knew where the damned thing was hidden. And it was hidden well.

Which meant that *thing* beating in Lucifer's chest didn't belong to him. Ursula had infected him with someone else's heart. A good heart. One untainted by Hell and its sins.

Absolutely catastrophic. It needed to be removed at once! Problem was, how did one remove the heart from a demon who probably wouldn't lie still while they cracked his chest open?

Gaia sighed as she leaned against the rock in the garden Lucifer had specially made for her in the middle of his castle. So sweet, even if he blustered and denied his intention.

"You made me a garden."

"No I didn't. It's just a useless space with rocks and shit that you can use if you like. Or not. I don't really care."

But he had enjoyed the reward. The memory warmed and saddened.

Would he ever take her over a rock in this garden again?

Her head drooped. She couldn't give in to defeat. She and Luc had gone through too much for her to give up on him yet.

I need to change my focus and concentrate on what is surrounding me.

The rock garden didn't have the lush greenery

of her Eden. It lacked the soft, susurrations and chatter of her plants or the sweet babble of a brook, but the whispery silence of shifting ash and stoic rocks had its own kind of soothing effect.

A whisper of a footstep let her know she was no longer alone.

"I unleashed the Lord," Neffie said, breaking the calming quiet.

"Did he go on a murderous rampage?" she asked, hopeful.

"He did not."

Hope dashed. "Was he at least mad about the exam we forced on him?" Gaia asked.

The sorceress snorted. "I wish. He thanked me for my concern and praised my work."

Dragging her fingers down the rough surface of the boulder, Gaia held in a sigh. "Nothing seems to bother him."

"He is a man at peace with himself and the world. A man no longer concerned with getting revenge."

"He's not concerned with anything anymore." Not even making Gaia feel like the most important woman in the universe.

Sure, Luc said all the right things and currently planned a lavish wedding to publicly declare himself as her one and only mate, but that man wasn't the one she'd fallen in love with.

Who are you kidding? The Lucifer I used to know dragged me kicking and screaming into love—and often to the bedroom.

"Put me down," she squealed as she pounded at his back.

His callused hand, hard from centuries of sword work,

and golf, dragged the length of her leg, pushing her skirts over her rump. "Not until we find a bed, wench," he declared in his most villainous pirate voice.

"Since when do we need a bed?"

Good times followed. Many of them, as a matter of fact. Enough that she couldn't help but fall in love. Even if she never wanted to.

People said she was obviously polluted to even think of marrying the rascally, foul-mouthed bastard, but there was something about Luc. Something about the way he made her feel…

He makes me feel young and beautiful and important and…

Not makes. Made. The man who inspired all those things was gone. In his place, a perfect gentleman. A perfect bore. She couldn't stand that man.

I want the old Lucifer back.

"So when should we rip that fake heart out of his chest and get him back to normal?"

A grimace twisted Nefertiti's features. "I wish the solution were so simple. I would have cracked open his chest, yanked that beating imposter from his chest, and devoured it right then and there if I thought it would fix him."

"But?"

"But I fear doing so will kill the Dark Lord."

A world without her dark lover? The very suggestion made the chlorophyll in her veins run cold. Gaia straightened. "What do you mean kill him? How would removing it be a problem? He survived without a heart before. Why not now?"

"Because right now his body needs it. A person can't just tear out the organ without preparation and spells and contingencies. Spells, I might add, that only *he* can perform. Something about that whole free will thing the universe forces on us. I almost guarantee, with the mood Lucifer is in, there's no way he'll be willing to tear that sucker out."

No, this weak imitation probably wouldn't. "So am I supposed to leave him like that? That's just cruel. Xaphan is right. He'd be better off dead. The Luc I know would hate to see what he's turned into." The Luc she knew would beat up the Luc he'd become. And she'd cheer him on!

"There is another option," Nefertiti offered in a slow, drawn-out tone.

"There is?" Gaia felt hope fluttering in her breast, a slender stalk trying to burst free from a seed.

"We need to replace his new heart with his old one."

"Use his old one? You do realize I don't have it."

"But you know where to get it."

Gaia did. "What you're talking about is pretty much impossible. I mean, there are layers of protection guarding it that are meant to stump even the most skilled of thieves." She should know. She'd helped designed some of them, and in return, Lucifer helped design some of the spells protecting her hidden heart. Between the pair of them, no one could get through.

"No one person could hope to survive, but what if you took a specialized team? A team of minions who'd do anything to free him?"

What if indeed…

*

Bang.

Once again, Gaia and all of Lucifer's most trusted minions—and family—gathered around the table in the Garden of Eden.

She didn't waste time. "Lucifer needs his heart."

"Funny because I thought the problem was he had too much heart," Felipe countered.

"But it's not *his* heart." Gaia explained their discovery to everyone. "So, Nefertiti thinks if we can replace the imposter organ with his true one then he might go back to normal."

"What do you mean might?" Muriel queried. "Will this work or not?"

At this, Gaia could only shrug. "Since we don't know if it's ever been done before, we can only assume."

"No. Not that word," Katie shrieked. "Because when you assume you"—everyone joined in—"make an ass out of you and me."

The ribald laughter, despite the serious situation, made Gaia smile. If anyone could help, then these nutjobs could.

But they deserved to know the whole truth of the mission. "I'm going to need volunteers. However, I feel I must warn that where we need to go is fraught with peril." Hands shot up. "Possible death." None of the hands wavered. "A chance you might never return home."

Not a single one of them changed their minds. Their loyalty for Lucifer would have made the new version beam and sniffle. The old one would have gagged.

As for Gaia, she could have hugged them all in that moment, but then they'd think she was afflicted like Lucifer and would probably lynch her. She wasn't as well liked as her fiancé. Probably better to go with a flat, "I guess you lot will do. Except for Muriel."

"What do you mean not Muriel?" Her daughter slapped her hands on the table, and she stood, eyes glowing, the flames of Hell reflected in them.

"You can't go because you're needed here in Hell. You can't expect us all to go traipsing off. Or did you want to explain to your father how you lost his kingdom because you wanted to play heroine?"

Shoulders drooped as Muriel sank back in her chair. "I hate you."

"I know. Now get over it and stop being a drama queen."

"It's prissy princess. And I will never get over it."

Muriel had abandonment issues. Justifiable ones, but that was a whole other story.

"So where are we going anyhow?" Valaska asked, the stalwart Amazonian always keen for battle.

"Dante's Inferno."

"The theme park in the seventh circle?" Mictain asked.

"More than a theme park," Gaia informed them. "That dangerous, never-ending roller coaster ride is the hiding place for Lucifer's dark heart. The treasure at the end of the quest."

"There's a treasure?" Katie straightened. "I like pretty treasures."

"Are you sure about that? According to Amazon legend, no one's ever made it to the end of the ride," Aella interjected. "And not for lack of trying."

Indeed the Amazon warriors had tried—and

failed. It was considered a rite of passage to attempt Dante's Inferno with badges of honor dependent on how far they managed to go.

None ever made it to the end, but then again, none ever had the advantage of Mother Earth on their side.

#cheatingforagoodcause

Chapter Six

@GaiaLuc4ever: A male must be strong and resist the impulses of the flesh. I know I can do it. #delivermefromtemptation

"LUCIFER. LUCIFER. Where are you?"

Sweet Gaia's voice called out from the other room, but Lucifer dared not answer. He couldn't let her find him.

I think she should see what you're doing. His inner voice, with his deviled horns, somehow took enough control to make him utter an, "Over here."

He slapped his hand over his mouth. Too late. She'd heard.

Appearing quite lovely in a diaphanous green gown, Gaia stood in the doorway. Shock stretched her features. "What are you doing?"

At her query, Lucifer sank lower in the frothy bubbles of his bath. "I am having a private moment."

"Tell me you're whacking off in there," she muttered.

"Most certainly not. Simply relaxing with soothing music and fragrant bath salts. I had a busy day with the caterers."

"The Lord of Sin does not take baths."

"Of course he does."

Only if there's a naked woman in it.

Before Lucifer knew what happened, he'd

reached out and yanked Gaia into the tub with him.

She uttered a squeal and landed with a splash—atop him.

Utterly appalled at his own actions, he sputtered, "Sorry. So sorry. I don't know what came over me."

Laughter bubbled from her, a giggle like he hadn't heard since their engagement dinner. She looped her arms around his neck. "This is more like the Luc I know." She rubbed her nose against his, and he returned the gesture. Nothing wrong with a little cuddling. They were, after all, engaged to be married in a few days.

That's it, buddy boy. Justify a little wink-wink-nudge-nudge.

Uh-oh, if his inner voice approved, then that meant he should deny the pleasure. He meant to set her away from him, but the small confines of the tub made it impossible, and her latch on him wouldn't relent.

The proximity did things to his body. Conjured carnal thoughts. For distraction, he tried counting duckies, smiling ones with little halos to remind him to be good.

She rested her forehead against his. "Do you remember the last time we were in a bath together?"

"No." Lie. The image came to him in living color.

Wearing only a robe, loosely belted, he sneaked into the bathroom, the one he'd had made for her with the massive Roman tub. He stood for a moment staring at the vision of loveliness. Gaia lay in the almost pool-sized tub, head tilted back, eyes closed, a layer of bubbles hiding the naked flesh of her body.

The robe fluttered to the floor as he shouted "Cannonball" and flopped into the water. He didn't care that waves sloshed over the side. And neither did she. Her lips clung to his, and her wet legs wrapped around his waist.

"You do remember," she whispered.

He closed his eyes against her piercing gaze as the memories flowed over him, but he could do nothing to quell the erection that pushed between their bodies.

Please don't let her notice it.

She squirmed. "Well, hello there, big boy."

Feel free to say hello with your lips, wench. Remember that thing she does with her tongue?

He did. So did a certain part of him, and it didn't care about respect or propriety.

Must resist. Lucifer pushed at Gaia, managing to roll her to the side enough that he could scramble out of the water, cheeks blushing as he flashed her his man bits. Even when he tucked the towel around his loins, he felt heat flushing his skin.

It didn't help that Gaia lay in the tub, skin dewy, lips tilted in a smile. "Hey, good-looking, why don't you drop that towel and come back in here?" She trailed a finger in the water. "It's still warm."

"I will resist temptation." He chanted the words aloud as he fled the bathroom. Not an easy flight and he couldn't even blame the voice in his head. It watched his flustered actions with a pleased smirk. It knew he'd almost given in to sin. It approved.

Come on. Indulge a little. I promise you'll enjoy it.

Ignoring the insidious whisper, he hurried to pull on his underpants—plain white cotton briefs, the kind respectable men wore. He'd managed to get his arms and head through the holes of his shirt when *she* appeared in the doorway of the washroom.

Gaia leaned against the jamb, dripping water on his floor, still wearing that pleased little smile. "Oh dear. Someone got me *wet.*" Her gaze caught his. "Whatever shall I do?" She pulled at the first button of her dress, popping it through the soaked fabric, a fabric that clung to her every curve.

He swallowed.

"I really should get out of these wet things." Another button. Then another, enough that the fabric parted, revealing the side and underswell of her full breasts.

He couldn't look away.

A roll of her shoulder and the sopping dress slid off, baring more skin. More buttons were set free, and the dress began to drag downward, pulled by the same gravity that graced the mortal realm.

Frozen in place, he could only stare.

The wet frock hit the floor with a plop, but instead of worrying about the mess, he found himself riveted by the shape at the vee of her thighs.

She noted his inappropriate observation and remarked. "Do you like it? I've been having my attendants prune it in the shape of a heart. For you. *All for you.*" She practically purred the words, and for some reason, his knees wobbled.

He sank to the floor in slow motion, still bereft of voice.

With hips that undulated with every step, she approached and stopped before him. His eyes were level with her midriff, but that didn't prevent the scent of her from surrounding him.

Cinnamon and apples. It made his taste buds water.

Taste her.

How he wanted to, and for a moment, he forgot himself. Forgot his vows.

He moved in closer and breathed deeply then blew out hotly. A shudder went through her, and her fingers threaded through his hair.

Our thick and lush hair.

The vain reminder snapped him awake, and Lucifer recoiled as if burned.

He scrambled from her. "Sorry. I don't know what came over me," he apologized.

"I can tell you what didn't come," Gaia grumbled.

"Here. Let me get you a robe before you catch a chill." He grabbed one from the hook within the closet and tossed it at her.

He didn't check to see if she caught it, but hurried to layer himself in armor, er, he meant clothes, before facing her again.

When he did, he realized the robe sat at her feet and she still stood naked.

Glorious.

Tempting.

He flipped himself around to look the other way. "You really will have to forgive me. I don't mean to be so disrespectful."

A heavy sigh met his apology. She sounded so disappointed. He couldn't blame her. He was disappointed in himself. She deserved better than a fiancé who behaved like a lecher and stared.

"We're going on a trip," she announced in the silence.

"When?" he asked, staring at a corner of fabric peeking from a drawer. Were those duckies on those boxers? He thought he'd gotten rid of all of them.

You can't get rid of my duckies for they are legion.

He ignored the evil laughter in his head in favor of Gaia's next words.

"We're leaving tonight."

"What? We can't go anywhere tonight." He whirled around, forgetting her nakedness. Lucky for him, she'd thoughtfully covered up.

All the better to peel off her later.

"We are leaving tonight. Within the next hour actually. So you might want to rethink the outfit you have on."

He peered down at his pressed ivory slacks and teal button-down shirt. "What's wrong with my outfit?"

"It will get ruined where we're going. Which, on second thought, is probably a good thing so keep it. But put on some comfortable climbing shoes."

Nothing she said made sense. "I'm sorry, cherry blossom, but while I appreciate your wanting some alone time with me, I'm afraid it will have to wait until after the wedding. So many things to plan. So many things still yet to do for our perfect-perfect day."

For a moment, her lips pursed and her eyes flashed with green fire. Then her expression smoothed, and she batted her lashes as her lower lip jutted in a pout. "But you have to come, Luc. It was supposed to be a surprise, but I can't keep a secret from you. Our friends have planned a marvelous Jack and Jill for us. You wouldn't want to disappoint them, would you?" She smiled, and for some reason, something about that grin made the noisy voice in his head chuckle and say, *Devious wench.*

Of course Lucifer didn't want to disappoint his

friends. A Jack and Jill to celebrate his upcoming wedding. How thoughtful of them.

Bloody bastards cheated me out of a stripper bachelor party, whined the voice in his head.

Stuff it. A man about to get married had no need to see women removing their garments.

There is always a need to see jiggling titties.

In a few more days, the only breasts he would respectfully admire would belong to his wife.

Ack. Argh. Choke. The horror.

The whining lasted the entire trip and only cut short when Gaia removed the blindfold from his eyes. As his closest friends and family shouted surprise, Lucifer couldn't help but stare.

This was their idea of a Jack and Jill? An amusement park?

Welcome to Dante's Inferno flashed in red, blue, and orange neon while also shooting purple sparks that fizzled in the air. The ominous hole into the mountain brought a shiver, especially when the metal cars came rattling up the track and stopped, waiting for them to climb aboard.

"Why don't you all go ahead, and I'll wait for you at the exit?" he said.

Pussy.

How about not in the mood to maim himself so close to the wedding.

Yanking on his arm, Gaia dragged him to the cart shaped to look like a swan—a twisted black metal swan with a flashing red eye.

"I just love roller coaster rides, especially ones with a little extra adventure, don't you?" Gaia asked. She shoved him through the small opening before she wedged herself onto the bench seat beside him.

The bar came down, much like the metal jaws of a trap. *Clang.*

With a jerk, the carts started to move forward to the exuberant yells of his friends.

They prefer the term minions. Evil minions to be precise.

The arched opening in the mountain loomed and then swallowed them.

Gulp.

#someoneholdmyhand

Chapter Seven

@GaiaLuc4ever: Whipping around in the dark, avoiding grasping tentacles, slashing scythes, and acid sprays. Whee. #adrenalinejunkie

THE DANK AIR IN THE mountain brushed her exposed skin as the metal carts clacked along the rail. The beauty of Dante's Inferno was no two rides were ever the same, as mechanisms at the rail forks constantly flipped and switched, jerking them left, right, and sometimes straight up or down in defiance of the laws of gravity.

Add to that the various deadly chambers they passed through and there was a reason why no one ever survived the ride to the end.

As a bit of a thrill seeker, Gaia quite enjoyed all the action, but her pleasure in the wild ride didn't stop her from clinging to Luc, squealing and laughing as they traveled the whirls and twirls. He, on the other hand, remained stoic and stiff. And not the kind of stiff she could wrap a hand around.

The new version of Lucifer didn't enjoy the exhilarating rush of the roller coaster. Nor did he take advantage of the darkness to cop a feel.

So she did. She squeezed his junk and was rewarded with a yelp.

"What are you doing?"

"Making out with you," she whispered against his ear before nipping it.

"We need to pay attention. This ride is dangerous."

"I know. It's such a turn-on." She rubbed his crotch, feeling a triumph spurt of warmth when his cock began to show signs of life.

Their rattling train went soaring over a break in the track, but she paid no mind to the abyss glowing orange with molten lava.

Squeeze of his bulge. A lick of his lobe.

A tremble went through him. "You shouldn't be doing this." He said it, and yet a heavy hand flattened itself atop hers, holding it in place.

They hit the other side of the chasm with a jostle and a scream of excitement from one of the cars behind them.

It took some maneuvering to get the cars all linked together. Usually, only one cart at a time shot into the labyrinth, with only a single occupant or cuddling couple. But this was an emergency, hence the daisy chaining of the carts.

So far, they'd managed to keep everyone on board. But the voyage was still young, and they now entered the Valley of Death. Ghosts, spectral spirits with eerie moans, and ectoplasmic glowing green blobs swooped and dove at their party.

A headless horseman on a charging steed of mist came toward them.

Lucifer yelled, "Duck!"

Her Lord ordered so she obeyed, managing to shove against the bar enough that her face ended up in his lap. A perfect spot and not an opportunity she'd waste.

She opened her mouth wide on the fabric of his pants and blew hotly. He might protest, "No. Stop that," but his shaft certainly didn't want her to. It expanded.

She might have taken things further, but Valaska yodeled from the head of the train, "We're coming to the Cavern of Webs."

In other words, the lair of the eight-legged freaks. Spiders, and yet spiders taken to a new, horrendous level.

Raising her head, Gaia had a moment to muster an energy shield before they were tearing through the silken veils. The sticky webs disintegrated at the touch of her power shield, but other occupants in their group weren't so lucky. She heard more than a few gags and sputters.

"Heads up!" Remy warned.

A fireball, trailing streamers of red and yellow, flew overhead and ignited a cluster of hanging threads. The fiery display came courtesy of Ysabel, the witch, who drew the flames from her fire demon mate.

The path ahead cleared as she lobbed ball after ball of flame, leaving only ash to sift down. The lack of webs revealed the true danger. Arachnids with multi-faceted, jewel-like eyes, clacking mandibles, and hairy purple legs. The creatures dropped from the ceiling on threads as thick and strong as steel cable.

With yells of excitement, the warriors in their group shoved free of their lap bars and stood in the carts, slashing and swinging at the jabbing legs. Nothing like a bit of danger to get them excited.

Usually, Lucifer would have joined in the revelry, his mighty sword in hand—a sword forged of the darkest sins, not the one in his pants. The true

Lucifer would have joined in and mocked his minions with his greatness.

This shadowy version of the Dark Lord sat huddled on the bench clutching the bar.

It sparked her annoyance. "Aren't you going to help?"

"I can't, the cart is still moving. I could fall out."

With a growl of annoyance, she smacked him in the back of the head. "Man up! Kill something."

"But they're icky," he said with repugnance, trying to wipe a sticky remnant of web from his pants.

"Then blast them with your mighty ire."

Big eyes regarded her with a woebegone expression she'd never expected to see on his face. "How can you ask me to destroy them when they are living creatures who are just doing what nature intended?"

He had not just said that. Lucifer, advocating a non-violent solution?

No. Just no.

Most people spoke of the fire that shone in Luc's eyes when his emotions ran high, but most failed to mention the green turbulence in hers when her temper got riled. "Since you like the spiders so much, how about one as a pet?" Twirling her finger in the air, she created a mini vortex, one that caught a dangling strand with a cat-sized arachnid on the end. Just a baby really, but perfect for her purpose.

With a scissoring motion, she snipped the silken cable and dropped the eight-legged freak into her fiancé's lap.

The scream he uttered trebled off the charts—and proved very unmanly. Yet, it did have an effect. So shrill did he shriek that the attacking spiders paused in their attack, and then, one by one, they burst.

It wasn't pretty. Or gentle. Or dry…for everyone else. She managed to pop a shield around herself.

Purple ichor covered the group, and for a moment, stunned silence froze their voices.

Then, as one, his minions shouted, "All hail the mighty spider slayer, Lucifer."

And while Luc blushed and ducked his head at the praise, she couldn't help but note his bearing seemed a little straighter.

#ishestillinthere

Chapter Eight

@GaiaLuc4ever: Hope my inadvertent murder of the spiders doesn't make it rain on the big day. #sorry #needsadrycleaner

AS THEY PASSED FROM the now empty spider lair into another section of dark tunnel, Lucifer slumped in the seat.

Chin up, bucko. You were the star back there.

More like murderer.

Exactly. You showed those bugs who is boss. And you liked it.

Lucifer wanted to deny it, but then he would be lying. A part of him had enjoyed the rush of power as it blew out of him. Basked in the adulation of his friends, and the glowing thanks in Gaia's eyes.

It's called pride. Nothing wrong with that.

Except for the fact that pride led to other sins.

"Blowjob for your thoughts," Gaia murmured against his ear.

Accept the offer!

"No need for bribery. I was just mulling over the fact I lost control back there."

"Or finally regained some," she countered. "When are you going to admit the real you is the guy we saw back there?"

He shook his head. "No. That man is a killer. A demon without conscience."

"Exactly, and that guy is the Lord of Hell we all know."

"But he's bad." Wasn't he?

As if reading his doubts, she replied, "Would a bad guy have so many people want to come on this quest?"

"Quest? What quest?"

Gaia bit her lip. "I meant join on us on this marvelous Jack and Jill adventure." She uttered a high-pitched laugh that he recognized as false. "Just a bunch of friends showing us a good time before our wedding."

Since when was it a good time to try and kill the bride and groom?

Kill? Bah. As if a mere amusement park ride could manage that.

The train rocketed from a tunnel into a new room, brightly lit with overhead lights and wooden cut-outs made to resemble an Old West town.

For some reason, he felt his senses dull. The constant tickling on his skin and the static pull on his hair vanished. It was only when Ysabel moaned, "We're in a magic-free zone," that he grasped why.

"Incoming," Adexios announced.

Arrows whistled at them from rooftops, and slingshots fired rocks at their party too.

Gaia squeaked and hid behind him. How wrong was it that he wanted to squeal and hide behind her too?

I might just die of shame. The horned duckie mind sank in despair.

Most of the missiles clattered harmlessly against the metal boxcars, but a hail of rocks managed to pepper Xaphan and Katie.

"You did not just do that." With a bellow of rage, Hell's psycho leapt from her car and charged at the wooden façades. With a shrug and an, "I better stick close," Xaphan followed, unleashing his mighty sword.

Between the pair of them, they managed to deflect most missiles while making their way closer to those firing. Meanwhile, the track looped on itself, a switch having set them in a closed circuit. Around and around they went, every pass keeping them in the target zone.

"Shouldn't someone aid them?" he ventured.

"Don't insult them like that," Gaia snapped. "Katie could handle these idiots by herself. Xaphan is just going along to make sure she doesn't get carried away and decide to clear the whole mountainside of traps. After all, Dante wouldn't be too happy if we broke his roller coaster. It took him centuries to perfect it."

Indeed, Katie could clear the area by herself. With her blonde pigtails bobbing, she weaved in and out of the wooden façades, popping up briefly to send a cloaked imp falling to his screaming death.

As for Xaphan, he twirled his broadsword, protecting the train whipping in its roundabout from missiles.

When the last arrow fell to the ground, a loud click sounded, and the track switched lanes, sending the train hurtling onward…leaving two of their number behind.

"Shouldn't we go back for them?" Lucifer yelled as the wind tried to rip the words from his mouth.

"They'll be fine. Besides, we've been gone long

enough they're probably in full-on celebration mode."

"And?"

"And, given you're such a prude these days, you might not want to see it."

"Oh." *Oh.*

We should totally go back. Nothing like being a demon on the wall and watching to get a little something-something happening.

Again, he wanted to deny the implication he enjoyed a bit of voyeurism, but he couldn't help recalling the times—the many, many times—when he'd floated a few stories high and peeked in some windows. Although, of late, he preferred to spy on his lovely fiancée as she pleasured herself—then, with a wink, invited him into her boudoir and pleasured him.

"You're blushing again," Gaia noted.

"No, I'm not." The lie came too quickly to his lips. He clamped them tightly, lest his tongue betray him again.

Wind whistled past his ears, cooling the tips as they whipped onward. Faster and faster. The train barreled into the unknown, and yet he would have said that wasn't why trepidation filled him. The end of the journey neared. A part of him knew this, and for some reason, it nagged at Lucifer.

I know why. But I'm not telling.

Which worried him most of all.

#mightneedanexorcism

Chapter Nine

@GaiaLuc4ever: Getting close to the journey's end and have yet to kill irritatingly polite devil. #couldchangemymind #rideisnotdone

THE JOURNEY SEEMED to take forever, and given the time looping in Dante's Inferno, that was a distinct possibility. The ride sat in a pocket outside reality, abiding by its own quantum rules about space and time. For all intents and purposes, not even a second passed in Hell or the mortal plane while they rode the wild train.

Yet, all things eventually came to an end, an immutable fact that seemed prevalent no matter what dimension they resided in.

With fewer minions than when they started, and a much shorter section of carts, at last they rattled to a stop outside the chamber that was their final destination.

A bedraggled crew of minions disembarked, worse for wear but grinning wildly because of it. The general vibe in the room was one of accomplishment and even fellowship. By working together, a feat almost unheard of in Hell, where it was every demon and creature for itself, they'd managed to make it through all the challenges.

Now, only one major test remained. Actually finding Lucifer's heart.

Not that the flashing sign for this final destination advertised this fact. In bold neon letters, which dripped ectoplasmic blood on the floor, it announced

Chamber of Choices. Make your pick. But choose wisely…

The choice, however, was anything but clear.

The room appeared cavernous, stretching at least one hundred feet overhead and twice that across. Chiseled from the deepest obsidian stone at the heart of the mountain, the room absorbed the torchlight that flickered from sconces. The burning oil hazed the room in a smoky shadow, as if the room needed more mystery. One only had to gaze upon the thousands of honeycombed holes peppering the wall to instantly wonder what was inside.

For some, inside some of those holes there existed a way out, a lever that, when pulled, would send them sweeping to the exit. It would expel them with fireworks and grand horns proclaiming them masters of Dante's Inferno, supposing, of course, the lever actually worked. None had ever reached it before.

But only a small handful of holes had this escape mechanism. Inside the others…gruesome death or painful injury. Not the permanent kind. Apparently, killing off patrons was bad for business.

In this dimension, while riders could die, they always returned home intact, much to the irritation of the Amazons and Valkyrie. Apparently, they wanted to keep the scars.

Not interested in escape or one of the thousand ways to die, Gaia looked around for a clue as to the whereabouts of the item only she and Luc knew was hidden in this place. An item Luc didn't want her to find.

Brushing his hands down his ready-for-the zombie-apocalypse outfit, Lucifer joined her. "Well, now that we've made it, how about we find the exit lever and get out? I could use a bubble bath."

The disgusted look on her face brought a stain to his cheeks. Embarrassed? He should be. "A bath? After battle you usually want to fuck." And fuck well, she might add.

Nothing like the adrenaline from a good fight to fuel the home fires. She'd never made it so long with her skirts down after such a good run.

"No need for vulgarity, my enchanting soon-to-be queen. A pretty mouth like yours is—"

She couldn't let him finish. If she did, she might just punch him, so she spoke first, using words the real Lucifer would. "Good for sucking dick. Is this a hint to get on my knees?" She cocked a hip and licked her lips.

He huffed. Literally huffed and flounced off. She resisted the temptation to throw her shoe at him, especially when she noted her actions being recorded.

A certain reaper noticed too. "What the hell are you doing?" Mictain hissed in Marigold's ear.

"Videotaping," replied the witch most nonchalantly. "If the old Lord comes back, I'll need leverage to get that temple I've had my eye on."

His brow arched. "You're planning blackmail?"

"Yes. If the Dark Lord returns, he and my dad will be so proud."

Yes, Lucifer would beam with pride at being blackmailed, even as he scrambled to get rid of the embarrassing video clip. Murder and starting a war with Zeus, Marigold's father, would also be possible scenarios, but scenarios that would happen only if the old Lucifer returned.

If they found his dark heart.

Not if. When.

"What are we doing here?" Niall asked, his kilt and combat boots having survived the trip but not his shirt. Aella had torn that from him after the first battle. She remarked, "He's not bad to look at for an old guy." To which Niall replied, "I'll show you old." Unfortunately, something had attacked before he could flip his kilt and prove his vigor.

"We're here because this is our final destination."

"Destination to where?" Now that Niall had made it through the death-defying gauntlet, he relaxed. Relaxation meant he'd flipped his sword so the point hovered an inch or so off the ground and made a few practice swings where he aimed at the holes in the wall.

Knocking things into the crevices wouldn't help them find the treasure.

"Not where. Why," Gaia corrected. "We are here to retrieve Lucifer's heart. It's in here. In one of those openings."

"Fuck me, there's like thousands," Remy exclaimed. "How are we supposed to find the right hole?"

"That's not usually a problem," snickered Ysabel.

"You take the thousand to the left. I'll take the thousand to the right." Aella pointed at the group, delegating, but Gaia held up her hand and shook her head.

"No need for that. I can find it."

"You know which one holds it?" Mictain asked.

"Not exactly." Even Lucifer didn't trust her that much. Actually, he trusted no one, so not only did he not let her, or anyone else, see which hole he hid it in, a powerful magic spell added another layer to keep the heart from those seeking it. "As part of its protection, Lucifer's heart moves location from hour to hour, sometimes minute to minute." There was no map or special sequence to its random reassignment.

"Then how will you find it?" Felipe asked with a sniff to the air. "There's no scent in this place. Not even our own. No markings, no sound. At least so I assume. Do you hear anything?" he asked Jenny. Jenny, the daughter of Ursula, with a voice that could kill. Quite literally. Most of the time they kept it under control with an amulet meant to nullify its effects. Those who were utterly tone deaf, like Felipe, had no problems.

But those folks were rare, and having lost her protective amulet while singing some four-armed titans into clubbing each other in one of the caverns, Jenny just nodded her head. A good choice, lest she manage to get some of them to commit seppuku.

"Seems kind of impossible," Felipe said. "And this from a curious cat."

"There are other senses we can use to find it," Gaia intoned in her best Mother Nature voice. Ominous words helped build the legend, or so Lucifer kept insisting.

How I miss you, Luc.

Not for long, though. She could get him back. She just had to find his heart.

Taking in a deep breath, she closed her eyes

and let herself relax, head tilted back, only to tense as Lucifer said, in a voice soft with a hint of sadness, "You don't want to do this. Leave it be. No good will come of it."

"Which is why I have to do this," she replied. Good had no place in her lover's body.

Arms spread, eyes tightly shut, and senses reaching, she looked for the seed, the teeny-tiny seed she'd shoved in a corner of the box for Lucifer's heart. A future precaution so she could locate it in the event there was a need.

That need was now.

Funny how she originally planted the seed because she'd feared she might have to one day stop a rampaging, out-of-control Dark Lord. But instead, here she was seeking his heart to return his wicked side to him.

Where are you, my little seedling?

Gaia didn't react to the yelp as a curious kitty stuck his paw where he shouldn't. She ignored the hollers of, "Holy shit, what's that climbing out of the hole?" She let the noise of the minion crew as they battled the catacomb's defenses fade as she sought out the spark of life she'd left behind.

Many people saw seeds as inert items. Dead until planted in soil and nurtured. Wrong. Seeds were life. And, as such, they could call to her.

Speak to me, my little one. Where do you hide?

Wink.

With eyes still shut, she pivoted toward the slight tremor.

Blink, blink.

The tiny beacon called to her, and she followed, her feet floating from the ground, the call of her seedling guiding her.

Opening her eyes, she noted she hovered in front of a section high off the floor. An array of holes faced her, but she knew which one she needed.

In plunged her hand, up to her elbow. Not far enough. She pushed deeper, the jagged rock tight around her flesh, unyielding. But she knew this was just another ploy, a trick to keep the unwary from finding its precious secret.

The very tips of her fingers touched cold metal. Shoving her arm into the hole as far as she could, she managed to curl her hand around the object and slowly pulled it free.

Although not eager to relinquish its prize, the rock yielded, letting her bring forth the treasure box.

It snagged only at the entrance, one last-ditch attempt to hold on. "Oh no you don't," she grumbled, giving it a firm yank.

The box tumbled loose. Clutching it to her chest, she let herself float to the ground, a falling petal amidst demons and witches and more, who formed a circle around her.

Lucifer didn't join them. The man sulked with his back turned, a petulant move so redolent of his old self.

No sooner had her feet touched the ground when she knelt, placing her precious burden on the ground, relief at finding it suffusing her—until she saw the broken lock.

The pieces of it hung in shattered metal chunks. With her othersight—a way to see things hidden to those without magic—she clearly discerned the zings of the spells once protecting it hanging in tendrils.

No. No. No. She didn't want to think what it meant. A sob erupted from her as she lifted the lid and saw the black satin-lined interior was empty.

EMPTY!

Sob. *Maybe it's the wrong box. Maybe I made a mistake.*

Wink. The little nudge had her glancing again. Her shoulders rounded in defeat. She'd grabbed the right container. Her teeny-tiny seed remained tucked in a corner, along with a lingering hint of the cold dark sea and a grain of sand, a clue as to who had taken Luc's heart.

"Ursula!" she growled. The sea hag had stolen Lucifer's heart.

And I am going to get it back.

#servingtentaclesoupfordinner

Chapter Ten

@GaiaLuc4ever: 2 days until the big day, and my bride is getting cold feet. What can I do? #needsomeslippersoflove

THE JACK AND JILL, which doubled as a sly bid to return Lucifer to his old ways—*the best way!*—left the merry band bedraggled. And, in the case of his fiancée, dispirited.

Her hair didn't have its usual sunshine highlights and green luster. Her eyes didn't sparkle with mischief or emerald light. Tattered clothing clung to her grimy body in shreds, stained and beyond repair.

We really should strip those off her. You know, because we're nice like that.

If it weren't for the lascivious grin trying to tug at his lips, Lucifer might have believed the lie. He refrained from letting his hands tear the rags. Tucked them behind his back in case they, once again, became possessed of a mind of their own.

Wandering hands aren't a bad thing, especially when they end up under our wench's skirt.

Given he found it impossible to disagree, he sat on his hands abruptly. "That was quite the adventure," he said, trying not to wince at his own false brightness.

That's it, buddy boy. Fake it. Let the sin in. I dare you to meet it with a grin.

He did not fake it. Enthusiasm in the pursuit of not worrying Gaia with his rather impure thoughts seemed noble.

Justification. Cough.

"Why, Luc, is that smoke coming from your ears?"

Indeed his internal furnace seemed to burn a little hot with ire. He needed to calm down. Return to his even serenity. "Nothing's wrong, dearest." The easily spoken white lie served only to increase his inner turmoil, and the smoke thickened.

For some reason, this seemed to make Gaia happy. A little spark entered her smile, and her lips tilted just a bit. "So what do you want to do now?" she asked.

I want to do my wench. I say we tear those things off her, clean her, make her dirty and then clean her again. So we can dirty her again. See what I'm saying?

He did, in living, flesh-toned color. Gulp.

His hands dropped to his front to cover his inappropriate reaction. "I think I'll just soak in a nice hot bath then maybe enjoy some tea before bed."

Nooooooo!

"Tea and bed?" Her nose wrinkled. "I'm too wired for that. Aren't you feeling a little"—her voice dropped an octave—"*frisky*?"

Wench, instead of talking, you should be stripping and getting to your knees. On second thought, we should get to our knees and thank her sweet apple pie for being so fucking hot on that ride. Our wench kicks some serious ass!

She did. "I should thank you for your valiant protection of myself and our crew."

Don't thank her with words, you idiot. Use your tongue!

"Thank me? I know a way you can thank me." Her lashes fluttered, and her smile turned sensual.

I know that grin.

Yes, he did. Two days. He had to wait two more days. Be strong. Resist. "I'm really tired. I think I'm going to turn in now." Before he did something he'd regret.

Oh, you wouldn't regret it. Neither would she.

"Bed?" Gaia shook her head. "It's way too early for that. But you go ahead. Relax in your bubble bath." Said with a sneer. "I think I'm going to hang at Nefertiti's place for a few hours."

The witch's tower? Tendrils of smoke curled from his nostrils. He didn't understand his agitation.

I'll tell you why we're agitated. You're worried because she's horny, all on account you aren't man enough to plow her. Now, this horny wench of ours is about to go spend time in a bloody harem full of partially clothed nubile men trained in the art of sexual pleasure.

Stop. Her.

Wait, that wasn't the voice suggesting it, but him. And the following words were also his own. "Don't you need to return to your place to refresh and rest yourself?"

Gaia peeked down at her disheveled ensemble. "You're right. Totally inappropriate for a visit. But I don't have the patience to hit the garden." She snapped her slender fingers and, in a blink, stood in a new outfit.

A much more revealing outfit than the torn one of before.

"I think you forgot some parts," he observed. "Like maybe a shawl." A great big woolly one that draped from head to toe.

The delicate sound of her laughter tinkled like bells, and her eyes lit with amusement. "It's much too hot at Neffie's place for that. I get so sweaty when I'm there." She winked as she turned around, her short skirt barely covering the curve of her plump ass. "Don't wait up." Another throaty giggle as she peeked over her bared shoulder, the halter-top exposing more than it hid. "Actually, I guess since you don't want us sleeping together until the wedding, you won't have any idea when I get back. Or what bed I'm sleeping in. If I can sleep. I've got so much energy."

With those words and a saucy bounce to her step, she left.

Go and drag that luscious ass back here and put her over your knee.

Why? She hadn't earned any punishment. Gaia had the right to visit whom she chose. He trusted her.

Never said we couldn't trust her. Woman is faithful, but that doesn't mean you shouldn't look for an excuse to slap that precious ass.

If only he couldn't remember the sound as his hand cracked a cheek, the pink color that infused it, and the way she moaned when he followed the tap with a lick of her flesh.

Good times. The evil voice sighed. *Pity we'll never get to enjoy being that close to her again.*

What did his sly subconscious imply? In less than two days, they'd become man and wife. Demon and Goddess. In two days, as part of his husbandly duty, he'd pleasure his wife.

Aren't you just the most naïve dreamer?

What was that supposed to mean?

Anyone can see the woman is going to bail on you. Can you blame her? She signed on to marry the biggest badass in the universe, and instead, she's getting you. Uttered with such disgust.

And wrong. Gaia was going to marry him because she loved him.

Your optimism is a lie. She will run. I've whispered in the ear of more than my fair share of skittish brides and nervous grooms to know the look.

What to do then?

Drag her back and give it to her good. Make her scream our name a few times and she'll forget all about running away.

More disrespect wouldn't help matters. He needed a proper way of handling this. He needed help.

Real men don't ask for help, snarled his inner duckie with eyes that glowed red and horns that curled over the forehead.

Ignoring the inner muttering, he mulled whom to call for advice, and it was immediately obvious. Who better to discuss his problems with about his wench, er, he meant his lady, than his daughters?

Laughter inside his head. *Oh this should be good.*

And then the voice he heard went quiet, but Lucifer could feel it watching, anticipation clear.

While Lucifer waited for his daughters to arrive, he took a fast shower. No bath yet, not with company arriving. He dressed in casual gray slacks, with a firm crease in the front, and an orange shirt with an imp embroidered over the place where his heart beat. It wasn't his first choice, but his Hawaiian selection seemed to have gone missing.

For some reason, he chose cowboy boots to complete his ensemble. Big, pointy-toed black ones with spurs that jingled when he walked. Also not exactly the most comfortable footwear.

But they look kickass.

They did. He tried to stomp the vanity that kept tempting him to peek at himself in the mirror. He still caught his reflection and admired it. He'd have to punish himself later.

The room Lucifer chose to meet his daughters in had a certain comfort to it, and yet it wasn't his style at all. Huge, to the point of obscene, the red rock walls were smoothed at least twelve feet from the floor and painted a metallic gray, and yet done in such a way that streaks of the red stone still peeked through.

A massive hearth took pride of place against a wall, the clear glass blocks lining it requiring its own team of imp polishers. But the ostentatious fireplace proved its worth with the mound of ice chunks heaped within that radiated a lovely chill to the room. A lavish expense in a place like Hell.

Set in a lopsided semicircle from the hearth, several pieces of furniture. A glass block table, which served as a scrying mirror for the times someone wanted to watch live television. There was a pair of couches also in the space, covered in a silky black and gray fur. Plus a table with two straight-backed chairs. A good place to play games.

And sturdy enough to toss the wench atop for a good plowing when she catches me cheating at the Game of Unlife and demands restitution.

As quickly as his mind veered into the dirty gutter, he steered back out. Easy to do by focusing on his daughters, who arrived and made themselves at home.

Bambi sprawled on a fur-covered couch with a leg flopped over the back. Thankfully, she wore leggings for once and didn't flash him any bits, so he decided not to reprimand her for the form-fitting shape of her leggings and the strip of skin exposed by her cropped midriff top.

"So glad you could both come," he said, clapping his hands together.

"Did we have a choice?" Muriel asked.

"Of course you had a choice. But I just knew my precious daughters wouldn't let me down."

Poor Bambi coughed behind him, and he wondered if she was coming down with something. Probably on account she didn't wear enough clothes.

"So why did you need us here?" Muriel asked.

"I think Gaia might not want to marry me."

"What makes you think that? Has she said something to you?" Bambi asked, not looking at him while her long, lacquered nails tapped at her hellphone.

"Just a feeling." He had so many of those lately. Was that the problem? Had Gaia caught onto his emotional mess? Did she think he doubted their love? Or was that other voice right? Did she not like who he was? "Has your mother said anything to you?"

"Nope." Not a very loquacious reply from Muriel. His youngest daughter sat at the table, her hellacious version of a laptop open, the horned duckie emblem on the lid glowing red. A house brand, and very limited too.

Electronics didn't run well in the pit unless you had access to excellent magic. Lucifer had the best.

"Cold feet are normal," Bambi said. "She'll be fine."

"Or not," Muriel added in an ominous tone. "You know I think this joining of yours is unholy. Why can't you just continue the way you are?"

"Isn't it time you overcame your issues with your mother for the sake of the family?"

"You want me to forgive her? You?" Muriel gaped at him then glanced at her sister, who shrugged. A second later, they both burst out into giggles. "Never," Muriel snickered.

"Little lamb is right. Forgiveness is for the weak. If they've betrayed you once, they might again."

"Sometimes people make mistakes. That doesn't mean you shouldn't love them."

Muriel peered at him over the top of her screen. "Never said I didn't love or care. But that doesn't give anyone who betrays me a free pass. Vigilance is part of our family motto."

As was deceit, vengeance, and destruction.

"I trust her," he said.

"Apparently not, because you called us to talk about your fears instead of talking to her."

"I don't want to bother her if you think they're unfounded."

"Actually, I think you are right. And if she does ditch you, then she's got good reason." Slamming the lid shut on her laptop, Muriel stood. "If you can't figure out why she's unhappy and fix it, then maybe she should run. Then again, why would she run when she can dance away her frustration using Nefertiti's new stripper pole?"

"Stripper pole?" The faint words emerged with a surprised lilt from Lucifer.

"Yeah, she just posted an image on her profile of her licking a chrome pole."

"Let me see," Lucifer growled.

Bambi kept the phone out of reach. "I don't think so. Stalking your woman online is for men who don't trust. Or are you implying you don't trust Gaia?"

"I trust her." How sour those words tasted in

his mouth.

"Then there's nothing to talk about." Flipping off the couch, Bambi approached and pecked him on the cheek—*Eew! Wipe it off!*

Muriel tucked her laptop under her arm. "I gotta go. Chaos is brewing at my house. Auric and the boys are bugging Tristan again."

"What did they do to your merman this time?" Bambi asked as she linked her arm through Muriel's.

"Flavored and colored crystals in the swimming pool out back."

"What did Tristan do to retaliate?"

Muriel chuckled "Oh he got them good. He…"

Since his daughters left through a portal, Lucifer didn't hear what Tristan had done for revenge, but he really wanted to know.

Why? I thought pranks were a no-no, along with eating artificial sugar.

Thanks for the reminder. He didn't need to know what Tristan had done. What he did need, though, was an answer as to what was wrong with Gaia. His daughters hadn't provided one, which meant he still had his dilemma. How to know if Gaia planned to leave him?

Who could he turn to for help?

How about someone she'd dated and dumped in the past?

Don't you dare call that smug goody-two-shoes.

Family was always welcome in his castle.

Even family that lusts after our wench?

#iwillnotkillherex

Chapter Eleven

@GaiaLuc4ever: What to do when your man isn't giving you enough attention? Go see some guys who will. #jealousyisagirlsbestfriend

LEAVING LUCIFER, NOT in the least debauched, totally ungroped and utterly annoyed, Gaia called a portal and deposited herself outside Nefertiti's tower. The good thing about being a bit of a celebrity? It meant, as she took the steps, one at a time, a scantily-clad butler hauled open the doors, granting her entry.

A less irritated woman might have noted the perfectly sculpted six-pack and the lean waist tapering in a vee, barely hidden by the skintight shorts. The curly throwback blond hair gave the butler a boyish look, as did his rakish grin.

All wasted because Gaia could think of only one man. One damnable man who showed a few signs of his old self. But a few signs weren't enough for Gaia.

I want my big, bad demon back.

As she followed the smooth gait of the butler—with an ass made for grabbing—Gaia found her attention drawn by some changes in Nefertiti's tower.

The once gloomy, smoke-stained, gray stone seemed to have undergone a whitewash, so bright that the spooky ambiance no longer pressed upon the spirit. Vivid murals depicting scenes from an erotic seduction to the most vicious of tortures—also sexual in nature—gave way to tapestries woven to appear as windows onto fantastical gardens. She found the one of the purple-surfaced planet with its twin moons in the sky particularly lovely.

As for the window covering, the thick red velvet panels, held back with brass cords, were gone and, in their place, filmy curtains of a crisp white. Gaia had to wonder how they stayed clean. In the pit, ash was a part of life. It coated everything in a dull gray. White didn't stay white for long.

Unless a certain determined sorceress used magic to keep it pristine.

What had happened here? Since when had Nefertiti gravitated to such a clean and pure décor?

Did she somehow get conned into joining the light side? Had Neffie gone good?

Snicker. She highly doubted that. Still, she wondered about her friend's sanity level.

The new décor extended into the harem itself, the immaculate white offset with silver and the occasional hint of gold. And it was here that Gaia finally caught on to the decorating brilliance that Neffie had stumbled upon.

With such a pale canvas acting as a backdrop, it lent a certain eye-opening aspect to the men strutting around in little to nothing.

Oh my.

She was a woman, one still in her prime. One who could totally admire a perfect male form. She could also find herself a little dumbstruck when visually bombarded with more than a dozen at once. There were partially nude bodies everywhere, running a palette of colors from the finest ivory to a deep ebony to a milk chocolate shade in between. She even spotted a purple and blue fellow.

The half-dressed men wandered about, completely at ease in their bright loincloths. Their presence added quite the punch when viewed against the blank canvas of the room.

"Effective, isn't it?" said Nefertiti. She lounged on a divan, wearing a long red gown, slitted up both thighs. Her dark, glittering eyes watched as a man, with excellent thigh-muscle control, clung to a stripper pole upside down.

As for what he did on the pole… While not a prude, Gaia still averted her gaze. She had enough issues with Luc to compound them by drooling over her friend's man.

"I didn't realize you'd taken an interest in the exotic dancing art?" Keeping her back to the sinuous hump of the new objet d'art, Gaia approached Nefertiti. A line of divans and comfortable chairs circled around the pole, offering plenty of angles to watch from.

"Gaia, my dear friend. Come sit beside me." Neffie patted the cushion on the couch, and Gaia joined her, plopping down heavily.

The faux wood creaked. She smirked. Imitations were never as good as the real stuff. "I see you redecorated." She tilted her head to the left and noted more change, the orgy in the middle of the bathing fountain replaced with a waterfall with strategically placed flat rocks. How practical. She'd have to ask Neffie who designed it. The rock garden at the palace could use one.

"Do you like it? I woke up the other morning

and thought, it's time for a change. Shadowy halls and gloomy corners were so sixteen hundreds."

"I actually really do like it, although I am wondering how hard it was to get a pole that long." Gaia tilted her head back to see the newest craze stretched high above to a ceiling at least a hundred feet overhead. She also noted more dancers higher up on it, as well as a few men doing trapeze. Naked.

Oh my.

I wonder if Lucifer would want to try that.

The old Luc would have taken it as a challenge—*Watch me defy the laws of gravity, wench.* The new Lucifer would probably faint.

Sigh.

"Why the sad sound?"

"You must have heard about the missing heart at the end of Dante's Inferno."

"Yes. A most unexpected turn of events. But not the end of the world. That isn't coming for another fifty or so years, depending on the paths some mortals take."

Gaia blinked. The sorceress had a habit of throwing out tidbits like that. Most of her predictions never came to pass, as the future held many forks, and many pivotal events rested on the tiny decision of one.

However, who cared about the possible annihilation of mankind? Gaia had more important things to worry about. "I don't know what to do about Lucifer."

A moue of distaste curled Neffie's lips. "Yes, the Dark Lord is a bit irritating with his do-good mannerisms. Can you believe he asked me to disband my harem and stick to just one man at a time?" Nefertiti shuddered. "Perish the thought. That would be like asking us to only eat one chip. Or a single bite of a decadent sundae."

Personally, Gaia had her hands full—quite literally when erect—with one man. But Nefertiti's magic relied on sex, lots of it, hence her view on the matter tended to skew in another direction.

"I don't know if I can marry him, Neffie. I mean, the wedding is less than two days away, and whenever I think of tying myself to the imposter wearing his body, I want to burrow deep into the earth and hide."

"Then don't marry him."

But that would mean breaking his heart, a heart he currently had, even if it wasn't his own.

"Is there any way we could get the old Lucifer back without finding his heart? I see occasional glimpses of him. It's like he's still in there but stuck."

"His wicked persona overshadowed by his do-good organ?" Neffie appeared thoughtful. "Possible. And, if true, then perhaps, over time, the darkness that belongs to the Lord of Sin will submerge the pure heart and take over again."

Perhaps over time? As Mother Nature, she might have the patience to plant a seedling and watch it grow to maturity, even if that took decades. But when it came to Luc… She shook her head. "I don't have time to wait. Hell is falling apart. Demons are running rampant. The number of escapees to the mortal realm has multiplied. Muriel is doing her best to retain control, but she doesn't have the hard, commanding edge of her father."

"I noticed things were even more chaotic than usual. And while a little chaos is acceptable, too much means more work for me, which means more sex, which means fun, but a pussy can only handle so much before it needs a rest. Chafing is real, my friend, and let me add, it is not fun. For either party."

"Neffie!" Gaia exclaimed. "Way too much info."

"I know, which is what makes it so fun." The sorceress smirked. "But back to your dilemma. How to draw the Dark Lord out if he is, indeed, still in there? How about tossing him in a pit with a few monsters? Maybe slay a few beasts. Shed a lot of blood. You know. Something to get that adrenaline going."

Gaia shook her head as she recalled his squealing on the roller coaster ride. "Tried that. It didn't really work."

"How about shagging him good?"

"I wish he'd let me. The man is determined to wait until we're wed."

"So seduce him."

"I've tried," Gaia grumbled. "He practically runs away each time. It's a little demoralizing to my ego."

At that, Nefertiti went silent for a moment. Her eyes lost focus as she stared at the spinning of the man high above, the length of silver fabric flashing and drawing the eye as he weaved and spun with it. Gaia startled when Neffie broke the silence. "How about appealing to his sinful side?"

"I thought I was with all the stuff I did."

"Maybe we missed one. What are the main sins?"

Easy. "Murder. Theft. Lust. Avarice."

Again, the sorceress got a thoughtful expression. "Getting Lucifer to kill didn't work so well, and I doubt we could get him to steal. He lusts but won't act on it, so that leaves avarice. A most powerful emotion when wielded right."

Avarice, the close brother to jealousy.

Jealousy…

Could the solution be so simple? If there was something Lucifer hated, it was someone poaching on his territory. Didn't matter what it was—power, owning more awesome toys, or someone screwing with his woman.

I am his wench.

But would jealousy still work? The old Lucifer hated anyone making eyes at Gaia. He went coo-coo like a clock on 'roids if anyone so much as stared too long. Would the new version give a damn?

Only one way to find out.

Grabbing a neon green drink from a proffered tray, Gaia tossed back the very tart apple liquid. Then three more in various colors—fireball, menthol, and toxic mite remedy—before attempting to get frisky with the stripper pole.

A few attempts to swing didn't go well. She ended on the floor, staring up at swinging balls with an urge to sing the song "Big Balls" by AC/DC. Neffie served a potent brew, enough so that, when Gaia got to her feet and staggered, a quake flattened part of the Rockies.

Better keep a closer hold on my earth-shaking power.

Since dancing seemed out of the question, Gaia wrapped her fingers around the pole, leaned close, and stuck out her tongue before asking in a slurred voice for Neffie to, "Take a picture and post it."

They ended up posting several. Videos too. The amount of views pinged rapidly, and yet no rampaging demon came to drag her out of the harem of iniquity.

No roar of rage sounded, vibrating the rings of Hell.

The tower wasn't invaded by the legion.

Not a single damned thing happened. Sob.

Lucifer just didn't care.

"Arghhhhh!" She uttered a primal scream because she cared and she was just drunk enough to do something about it. "I've had it! I am going to march back to his place and tell him what I think. No more Mrs. Nice Mother Earth."

"That was you being nice?"

"Sarcasm is best when I'm not so pissed," Gaia growled, pointing a finger at Neffie and her wavering double. She wished the sorceress would stop moving.

"I have to question your plan. Are you sure you should confront him right now? You're a little unbalanced."

"I might be a little drunk, that doesn't mean my feelings have changed. I can't marry Lucifer as he is."

With that determination, Gaia slashed her finger through the air and nothing happened.

"Let me help you," Nefertiti said. She snapped her fingers, and a rip appeared.

Gaia stepped into the portal and exited by Lucifer's castle. But not the place it used to be.

Sounds of fighting and the even stronger stench of fire—real fire, not the brimstone of Hell—filled the air.

The rioting and chaos had reached the inner circle and neared Lucifer's source of power. If something didn't happen soon, Hell would turn into a place of complete anarchy. The demons and other dark creatures inhabiting this plane could spill over onto the mortal plane. It would mean decades of war.

Millions of deaths. A destruction of the planet.

My planet.

So much relied on Lucifer returning to himself. Big stakes, and yet, while it might make her petty, she didn't care about all that. The fate of Hell and Earth meant nothing to her without the man she loved.

And it was time she confronted him about it. Servants pointed Gaia in his direction. What they didn't warn her about was that she would walk in on the end of the world.

Okay, not quite the end, but it was as bad as Hell freezing over.

"Honey bunches, you're home." Lucifer beamed at her from his club chair. He wore a knitted sweater with leather patches on the elbows. And where had he gotten those spectacles perched on his nose? But most incongruous of all…

"Are you playing Scrabble?"

"Indeed I am, with the most wonderful brother Heaven has to offer."

Elyon, as he liked to be called now, formerly known as Yahweh and the One True God by a few religious branches, beamed at the compliment. "Why thank you, Lucifer."

"My pleasure, brother dear. I can't understand why we don't do this more often. Your manners are impeccable."

"Because he's a prat," she muttered.

"What's that, love bunny?"

She pasted a fake smile on her face. "Just saying I'm surprised you haven't offered our guest refreshments."

"Goodness gracious. Where are my manners?"

Lucifer practically skipped from the room,

surely causing some souls to throw themselves in the abyss to escape the horror of it. He'd no sooner popped out of sight when Gaia dove over the table, sending the game board and its pieces scattering. She grabbed Elyon by his white robe and dragged him close.

"What do you think you're doing?" she snarled.

"I am spending time with my brother."

His clear blue eyes regarded her with absolute innocence. Knowing him, it was sincere.

"You and Luc hate spending time together. You can't be in the room together five minutes without you threatening to send down your army of light and annihilating his evil realm once and for all. Luc usually tells you his army will kick your army's ass and to get laid." A brotherly rivalry that had existed since Lucifer decided he didn't want to share Heaven with Elyon and chose Hell as his home.

The relationship between them had turned contentious at that point with a battle for souls starting, a fight that Lucifer won without even trying. Elyon's rules for entrance into Heaven were rigid and not easy to follow. The Ten Commandments truly covered all sin.

But that rivalry was nothing compared to what had happened when Gaia dumped Elyon for Luc. A tad her fault for dating the wrong brother first. But then again, the brotherly rivalry proved kind of hot when they went on a holy crusade against each other.

She didn't see any signs of a holy war brewing with their quiet game of Scrabble.

"I know that before things between me and Lucifer were kind of tense. But that was before. My brother has changed." Elyon clasped his hands and raised his eyes to Heaven, his home.

"You think?" she said in her most sarcastic lilt. Wasted breath.

"I rather like this new version of him. He kind of reminds me of myself."

She made a moue as she shoved Elyon back in his chair. "And that's the problem. There's a reason I dumped your ass for Lucifer."

"Because you couldn't handle my glory?" He smiled beatifically at her.

She dropped her gaze to his lap. "I prefer something that needs two handles and knows how to take charge."

Even with all the sin he'd seen and passed judgment on, Elyon still had the ability to blush like a schoolgirl.

"I don't know what my brother sees in you."

Gaia sometimes wondered as well, and yet, for all their volatile dating in the past, they couldn't seem to stay away from each other for more than a few decades at a time.

"You need to help me fix Lucifer."

Elyon shook his head, his long white locks flying. "Why would we do that? I quite like him as he is now."

"Because, you short-sighted idiot, his whole goody-two-shoes bit has upset the balance of good and evil in the world."

"The forces of light are seeing the scales tip in our favor. I'd say that's a good thing for everyone." Scary part was God truly believed it.

"No, it's not a good thing. All things require balance. It's how nature works. If something skews too much one way, the whole ecosystem collapses.

Same thing with Heaven, Hell, and the mortal realm. We need a Lord of Sin."

"I thought my niece had taken over his job?"

"She did, but she doesn't have the special brand of evil needed to lead the army of darkness." But Muriel did try. Unfortunately, she'd succumbed to the pressure a few times and decimated a portion of the army.

"Surely you can find another sociopath to help out your progeny."

"You don't get it. You can't just replace Lucifer. He is one of a kind."

Dishes hit the ground with a clatter and crashing of porcelain. She whipped around in a froth of green skirts to see Lucifer staring at her.

His eyes shone. His arms opened wide. The smile on his face practically split his head in two. "Pookiekins, that is the most beautiful thing you've ever said. I think you're one of a kind too. Come here and give me a big smoochie."

She found herself propelled forward, Lucifer's beckoning fingers drawing her much like a magnet did with metal. A moment later, his arms wrapped around her in a gentle hug. No more rib crushing from him. The kiss he bestowed was soft and gentle too. No passionate plunder of her lips. No sinuous foray by his wickedly long tongue.

It was also short-lived, a tease of an embrace, and then he set her away from him.

With a snap of his fingers, the tray he'd dropped reformed and balanced on his palm. With a whistle and a swagger that needed more bad to make those pants work, Lucifer rejoined his brother.

Looking at the two of them conversing, she

was reminded of something Nefertiti had told her many years ago over a different round of drinks.

"Jealousy is a magic all its own. If properly set, it can prompt men to do just about anything."

The pictures she'd posted hadn't worked, possibly because no one had showed him.

Or he doesn't care.

She refused to believe that. She had to find a way to draw her evil overlord from where he hid inside because she knew Lucifer was still in there somewhere. She kept catching glimpses, despite the purity of his false heart.

If only she could coax that side of him to the surface. Surely if anyone could possess his own body, it was her Dark Lord.

Give him the right incentive.

In person, not via social media. Time to ignite the fuse that would turn on the tap for his covetous side.

"Do you mind I join you boys?" she asked brightly.

"Of course, lovely lady. Have my seat," Elyon graciously offered.

Looking utterly startled that his brother had stood first, Lucifer followed, but she'd already turned a smile onto Elyon. "Thank you. That is so kind of you."

What wasn't so kind was her intentional trip and fall into the heavenly deity. She hit him and clutched at his white robe. His hands steadied her. She remained close and peered into the visage of her bearded ex-boyfriend. But not lover. Elyon respected her too much for defilement.

"Oops. Clumsy me," she said with a giggle.

"No harm done," he said, clearing his throat with a small cough.

"I hope I didn't damage your robe." As she smoothed her hand down the fabric, she caught a whiff of smoke.

She bit her inner lip, lest she giggle. It was working.

"Robe is fine," Elyon managed to say in a strangled voice.

Tented, too, and Gaia made sure to whirl away in such a way that Lucifer noted it too.

A quick glance showed that smoke curled from Lucifer's ears and nose, but just in case he needed a little more nudging, she bent over right in front of Elyon.

"I should check my shoes. Maybe it was a loose lace tripping me."

Not very subtle as ass waggles went, but it resulted in Luc, in a tight tone, reminding, "You are wearing sandals."

"Goodness me, I am." Titter. She straightened. "You know what, instead of me stealing your seat, why don't we share it? Luc says sharing is caring." She shoved Elyon into the chair, the back of it hitting his knees and buckling them. He sat down hard, and she plopped onto his lap before turning a beaming grin on Lucifer. "Why don't you boys keep playing your game? You won't even know I'm here."

Lucifer certainly did know she was there, and smoke literally billowed from his ears. "I think Elyon and I were done. Didn't you need to return to your heavenly abode? It's getting late."

A hesitant hand came to rest on her hip, and Gaia didn't slap it away, not when its appearance turned Luc's face such an interesting shade of red.

"No rush to leave. I can stay a little while longer."

"Luc is right. It is getting late, and I really should get to bed." She fluttered her lashes so strongly a kaleidoscope of butterflies on the mortal realm took wing. She stood, but didn't move away from Elyon. His hand remained on her hip.

Lucifer's gaze watched it with burning intensity. But no laser beams yet.

"If you're leaving, then why don't I, um, escort you?" As Elyon stood, he finally removed his hand so he could offer the crook of his arm. She never did manage to grasp it.

Luc vaulted over the table and grabbed Elyon's arm. He propelled him in a quick forced march to the door.

"No need for you to put yourself out, brother. I'll take *care* of Gaia."

Damned straight he would.

And when Lucifer whirled around, she showed him how she wanted that care to work.

#tiredofwaiting

Chapter Twelve

@GaiaLuc4ever: Just over a day until the wedding. #mightnotlivethatlong #ballsaresoblue

FOR ONCE, THE SIGHT of Gaia's nudity didn't send him fleeing or covering his eyes.

Gaze wide open, Lucifer drank her in. Drank in every curve and nuance of her shape, a shape that undulated.

"What are you doing?" he asked.

Isn't it obvious? His inner voice snickered. *There's a reason why we're sporting wood, bucko. She's doing it on purpose.*

Surely she wouldn't?

Gaia stretched, arms over her head, arching her back and thrusting out her breasts. She pointed the toes of her feet and raised her leg. Up. Up. Until her toes pointed at the ceiling.

Damn that woman is flexible. Remember that time in her garden on the swing?

"You're doing it on purpose to seduce me," he blurted out.

"A prize to the devil who finally figured it out."

"You shouldn't be doing that. The wedding is—"

She cut him off. "I don't give a fuck about when the wedding is. I. Am. Horny." She stalked toward him, hips undulating, and he couldn't glance away. The movement proved hypnotic. Alluring.

Cock-hardening.

She stopped before him, the scent of her, cinnamon and apples, swirling around him in a heady mix.

Her hand shot out, and she grasped hold of his hair, a tight grip that she used to yank him close.

"Hello, lover," she whispered against his lips. "Long time, no see."

"What do you mean? We haven't been apart that long. Just a few hours." His heart hammered in his chest, and his breath stuttered.

Meanwhile, in his head, a certain voice crooned an old Madonna song.

"Silly devil. I mean been so long since I've seen your cock."

"Gaia!" He couldn't help a sharp exclamation of her name. Yet, he did nothing to move away. Nothing to remove himself from the sensual temptation she posed.

"L-u-c." She sang his name softly. "How much do you love me?"

"More than anything," Lucifer replied.

"Then prove it. Show me. Get to your knees."

Ordering us around? Don't allow it. Tell our wench to drop to her knees. Show her who is boss.

At her shove, he dropped, his knees hitting the floor hard, his face level with her tender parts. The heart shape of her pubes teased him, but not as much as her scent.

His mouth watered.

His fingers itched.

His scalp burned as she pulled on his hair and in a low growl said, "Lick me."

He would later justify his actions as something he had to do for his woman's wellbeing. She needed him, and even if it went against some of his principles, he couldn't say no.

But the truth? The truth was he wanted to taste her. Lick her and touch her.

He grabbed a hold of her thighs and parted them. He pushed his face between her legs, and his tongue eagerly sought her sex.

The tip of him touched those trembling nether lips and tasted the ambrosia of her arousal. So familiar on a certain level, and yet at the same time, it felt brand-new and exotic.

He explored her, his tongue slipping between the folds of her soft flesh. Probing her pulsing channel.

The sweetness of her arousal burst onto his tongue, exciting him. He spent a moment just tasting, reveling in her flavor.

While his body throbbed with urgency, he nevertheless took his time, even as her hands dug deep into his scalp and urged him closer. Pushed him. Begged him.

"More." The word kept coming from her in between pants and moans.

He gave her more. With the use of magic, he held her aloft as he slid her thighs over his shoulders. This exposed her even more to his hungry mouth.

The plushness of her ass filled the palms of his hands as he cupped it. He kneaded the flesh as he sucked at her sex.

When he finally left off tonguing her channel, she whimpered, "Don't stop."

He didn't intend to. He'd just changed focus.

Gaia cried out as his deft tongue found her clit.

Rub. Tug. Lick and nibble. He played with her love button, feeling it swell as her cries grew in pitch. The scent of her drove him wild, and his cock ached. Oh how it ached and strained.

But he would resist that ultimate temptation. This erotic moment he reserved for his woman.

Her pleasure is everything.

"Make me come." Her gasped plea let him know she'd reached that brink. As if he needed a clue, he could tell in the tautness of her body, the swollenness of her flesh.

The forked edges of his tongue came in useful as they split. While part of his tongue continued to flick her clit, teasing that sensitive nubbin, the other part jabbed into her sex, giving her throbbing channel something to grip.

And wow did she grip tight. She rode his mouth, a bucking goddess looking for nirvana, and he gave it to her.

Come for me, wench.

He felt it the moment she hit her peak, her whole body undulating while her satisfied cry echoed in the chamber.

In that moment, all his doubts and fears melted. This woman was his.

Mine.

Of course she would marry him. And now that he'd eased her sexual tension, she would smile again. Just like he would spend the next day smiling because, despite his throbbing cock, he felt such luck this woman wanted him above all others.

That kind of commitment deserved something from him. Something he never used to say before. "I love you."

#whydidsheslapme

Chapter Thirteen

@GaiaLuc4ever: Sex is great until your lover feels a need to talk. #justlookpretty #needsasmoke

CRACK.

Gaia couldn't stop her hand. No sooner had those inappropriate words left Luc's mouth—a mouth that had just acted much too dirty to say such a sappy thing—when she slapped him. And she wasn't gentle about it.

Frustrated much?

"What was that for?" he exclaimed, cupping the offended spot with his hand.

"You know why," she growled as she climbed off his shoulders. Big, broad shoulders that made a great spot to sit on while he did decadent things with his tongue. A tongue that then turned around and ruined a great orgasm.

For a moment, confusion reigned in his expression, then enlightenment dawned. "You're mad because I disrespected you and took advantage of you sexually before the wedding."

The warped reasoning spewing from him had her blinking. "Say what? Why would I be mad about that? I asked you to eat me." Totally worth it, by the way.

Once again, his brow furrowed. "I don't think I understand. On the one hand, you're saying it was what you wanted, but now you seem mad that I did."

"I'm not mad about you licking me to nirvana. Your technique is, as always, excellent. No, I'm mad that you ruined a fabulous orgasm by saying what you did after." She couldn't bring herself to say the words.

He didn't have the same problem. "I love you?"

Screech. To her, coming from his mouth, it sounded as if someone had taken sharp claws to the surface of her heart.

It also hurt. While it was childish, she couldn't help but clap her hands over her ears. "Argh. Don't say that. Stop it. I can't take it. This isn't you. The real you isn't nice. Or polite. The real you doesn't just give me an orgasm. He insists I give him one in return, maybe two. He talks dirty to me. He squashes me in bed, claiming there's not enough room just so he can pretend he's not snuggling. My Luc doesn't tell me he loves me. He doesn't have to. He shows it in the stupidest, most meaningful ways. That Luc is the real one, the one that I love. And, unfortunately, that's no longer you."

Tears burned in her eyes, tears she tried to blink away. A single one rolled free, trekking an anguished path down her cheek. It hovered for a second on the edge of her jaw before falling—and somewhere in the world, a deluge flooded the earth, the pain of her broken heart pushed onto the mortal plane.

Tonight, a part of the world joins me in crying.

More tears rolled, eager to cause their own natural disaster.

"Don't cry. I can't stand to see you cry." The fire in Luc's eyes proved at odds with the gentle compassion in his expression.

He should have yelled at her and told her to stop the waterworks. Luc should have promised to kill anything that was bothering her, plus their relatives. The funny thing she never told him was she thought him very gallant with his murderous offers.

This Lucifer reached out to touch her damp cheeks, to caress.

She flinched away. "Don't. Just don't. Stop all this kind and caring stuff. I can't handle it. I can't handle you." At least not at this moment with her emotions so raw.

The connection she achieved with Luc at the height of her pleasure, even if one-sided, always tore through the shields she used to protect herself.

I am mentally naked before you and unable to hide my fear that my Luc will ever come back. Would her dark lover be forever trapped? Was she doomed to only rare glimpses?

At his hang-demon expression, she whirled around. *I need space.* She stalked off, angry and—

Slam.

The sudden force of the grab propelled her until her back hit the wall. Familiar blazing eyes bored into hers. "Don't you dare walk away from me, wench."

Her mouth rounded into an O of surprise. How long since he'd used his term of endearment for her? Had he finally snapped free? "Lucifer? Is that really you?"

"I—" His face contorted. "Fuck off." He angled his head back as his eyes closed. The cords in his neck stood taut as he shook his head. "No. No. Stop it." Hands rose to cup his cranium. Still, he thrashed, a man possessed. Lucifer fought the imposter beating in his chest.

"Lucifer. Lucifer." She murmured his name as she tried to grab hold of him. Tried to offer him some sense of stability. But he danced out of reach and kept moaning, uttering the most nonsensical things.

"Stay back, you damned duckie. You will not have my mind."

"I will own it." Also spoken by Lucifer in a darker tone.

"Get back in your cage."

"Make me."

"How about I hug you?"

"Fuck off!"

He stumbled into the wall, having an argument with himself.

Remorse hit her. How hard and scary this split of personalities must be for her lover. Not that he'd ever admit it. Lucifer was arrogant like that.

But she wasn't too arrogant or unfeeling. As he huddled against the wall, she managed to trap him in her arms. "It's okay, Luc."

"No, it's not. You want to leave." He shivered, his imposter side in control again.

But for how long? The other half of Lucifer seemed to be gaining in strength. He resurfaced more and more often.

"I'm not leaving," she reassured him. Much as the situation frustrated her, she couldn't, and for several reasons. One reason could be summed up simply; 'til death do them part, in sickness and in health, part of their planned wedding vows. The traditional nature of it, spoken by the devil no less, was considered the height of blasphemy. Or so Lucifer convinced himself when she'd argued for something more formal than, "The wench is mine. Suck it, loser."

Tomorrow, she would say the words that bound them together. Forever. It didn't matter if they hadn't spoken the oath yet. She loved Lucifer enough to want to say them. In sickness and in health. She should live by them.

She had to treat his mental state as an illness. In that vein, she needed to find a cure. But she couldn't find a cure with him peering at her with sexy demon eyes.

"Let's go to bed," she suggested as she grabbed his hand. When he hesitated at her tug, she added, "Fully dressed." Since she was already nude, it was a simple matter to lift her arms and snap her fingers so that a gown would drift down over her in a cloudlike billow of fabric. Neck to toe. That should make him feel safe.

For him, she snapped her fingers and dressed him in flannel. Flannel covered in penguins sporting scarves. Shudder.

She clasped his hand between hers. "Let me sleep with you tonight, Luc. I just want you to hold me. I want to feel close to you. Please."

That word had him moving, following as if on a leash, letting her take him through various twists and turns to his large bedroom.

As they crawled into bed, she held in a sigh, mostly because Lucifer said, "I promise not to take advantage of you."

He's a sick man. Remind yourself of that when you feel an urge to slap him.

She should also make a list of all these times he said no to sex for when she mocked him later—if he got better.

He will get better.

True to his word, Lucifer spooned Gaia, kind of, but in a way that didn't touch her. At least an inch separated their bodies, a chaperone made of cushiony air.

Good because it meant, once he dropped off into a sound sleep—a sleep she enhanced with a bit of sleeping dust, a special blend only possible with fresh ingredients from her garden—she could leave.

She had business to attend to.

Wedding business. Lucifer needed a present, and she knew just what she wanted for him.

#fetchmeasilverplatter

Chapter Fourteen

@GaiaLuc4ever: Less than a day until we say I do. So much still to do. #bigdayalmosthere #squee

LUCIFER AWOKE TO a jangle of metal. Odd, because he'd cleared all the weapons and chains—of which he found many, some attached to the bedposts—from the room.

He pried open an eye then two. Both eyes staring, though, didn't change what he saw. "Morning, um…" He couldn't think of anything else to say, given all the blood in his body seemed to have pooled in one place. In his defense, he had good reason.

Gaia looked stupendous. A short green skirt showed off her long legs. Her utility belt cinched tight at her waist, making the curve of her hips more pronounced.

A pity about the armor hiding her beautiful tits.

A shame, indeed, along with the fact that she currently covered her lovely bare arms in polished green bracers. She paused and peered at him.

"You woke up earlier than expected." She finished off the last buckle and clicked her fingers. A strap appeared in her hand with a small dagger snapped to it. She buckled it to her thigh.

"What are you doing?" he asked Gaia.

"I'd say that was rather obvious. I am getting

suited up."

She's avoiding the real answer.

He didn't need his inner voice to recognize that. "Getting suited up for what? You're in battle gear."

"Of course I am. It's generally what one wears when going to fight."

"Fight who?"

Yeah who? I wanna go play too.

"Hell is at war."

What! "When did that happen?"

"Early this morning," Gaia informed him. "Rather abruptly too." Her lips curved into a smile as she pulled on thick green gardening gloves tipped with sharp metal points.

And this conversation was taking too long. "Hell went to war this morning? But how? I was sleeping." Didn't Hell going to war need some kind of approval by him?

I decide who will have the honor of being defeated by me!

The roll of Gaia's shoulder held an insouciance that made his inner voice scream, *Spank the naughty wench. She is totally asking for it with her saucy dancing around of your questions.*

He refrained.

"I declared war," she said with quite a bit of sinful pride.

That's my wench. We should totally spank her now for being a good girl. She's hot when she's bloodthirsty.

He quashed his inner voice. "You did what?"

In the midst of smearing green lines under her eyes and down her forehead in elaborate Celtic warrior whorls and lines, she tossed him a look over her armor-padded shoulder. "What else could I do? I could not let the insult go unpunished."

"What fucking insult?" The expletive blasted out of him, but he didn't apologize for it.

"Ursula has your heart. I sent that three-titted seawitch a decree demanding she hand it back. She refused. Disrespect is not to be tolerated, your very own words. And I don't like her. So I declared war." Spoken with more than a little glee.

"But you can't do that," he sputtered.

"Why not?"

"Because you're not the leader of Hell for one."

"That minor technicality didn't seem to bother Ursula or your minions. They are getting ready for battle as we speak."

"I don't approve."

"Don't you?" As she strapped her machetes to her belt, the blades sharp enough to split the finest grass, she strutted to him, a green goddess in warrior gear with her Roman sandals spiraling up her legs in metal bands also meant to deflect blows. Her features stood out in stark contrast as she'd pulled her hair taut into battle braids woven with green vine.

She came to a stop before him, and the scent of her enveloped him—apples, cinnamon, and impending violence. "Tell me you're not excited by the idea of confronting Ursula on the beach. Tell me you don't want revenge for what she's done."

He opened his mouth. Closed it.

If he disagreed, he lied. God, his brother, help him. She knew his inner darkness too well. He did feel a rush at the thought of a battle.

Kill the fucking sea hag.

Giving in to his bloodthirsty side would give it power. He had to stay in control. Had to remain focused on the important things. "We can't go to war today. We have a wedding happening tomorrow. So many tiny items need my attention."

Her look of disgust went well with the voice inside his head that muttered, *You fucking moron. She declared this war for you. For us.*

"Is this your way of saying you don't want to come?" Surely that wasn't a sly look in her eye?

Tell her we're coming. Grab our biggest fucking sword, throw on our Vader cape, and let's go kick some sea monster ass.

Instead, Lucifer said, "I cannot condone this violence. But since it's already done, I guess I can't stop it. Since you insist on pursuing this foolish notion that Ursula has somehow changed me, then you may take my army with you to keep you safe."

"I may?" She arched a brow, which, given her savage maquillage, proved somewhat menacing—and arousing.

The scent of her passion still clung to his skin. The memory of her cries, the feel of her against his tongue, possessed the ability to arouse. Tease. Tempt…

A good thing she had other plans and left. He might have been tempted to ravish her. As it was, he couldn't resist staring at the swish of her ass as she strode through the arch leading to the outside hall.

Go with her, you idiot. She needs us by her side to fight.

Fight? Fight a war she induced? A fight that could harm him—or harm her.

If anyone lays a single claw or tentacle on her…

They would regret it, which he could only ensure happened if he was by her side.

Lucifer called out. "I'm coming with you."

The declaration halted her exit from his room. She did a complete U-turn and walked back in. "What did you say?"

"I said I'm coming with you." Because cowardice was a sin, and letting Gaia march off alone just seemed plain wrong, even if he knew he'd encounter violence accompanying her.

What he didn't expect was for the violence to start at home.

Placing two fingers in her mouth, Gaia blew, and instead of the expected strident whistle, an ululating bird sound emerged. Boots clacked, a mini army of them, and snapped to a halt just outside his door.

A single figure entered dressed in black leather, so supple it didn't creak and yet ridiculously tough given it came from a dragon. The shit-kicking boots shone mirror-bright with a gleam attained by hours of spit polish, probably the task of a shoe shining imp. The almost impenetrable pants molded thick thighs sporting muscles formed over the course of years of training. A metal doublet of the darkest chromium rings fitted across wide shoulders. The face was covered by a helm intricately carved, the nose piece inset with runes while, from the back, a flame-colored plume dipped and wavered, even without a breeze, the magic within the feather charged and ready for battle.

Remy looked ready for war, and he knew it judging by his cocky smile.

He banged a gloved hand on his chest. "Reporting as requested, Mother General."

Mother General? The voice in his head went into paroxysms of laughter.

"Who's with you?"

"In the hall are Dante's group, Mother General."

"And the Dark Lord's other privileged minions, where are they?"

"They've gathered in the outer courtyard and await your orders, as does the grand sorceress in the barracks."

Gaia tucked her hands behind her back. "The army of darkness is ready to fight."

"They are ready to win, Mother General."

During this, Lucifer remained quiet, mostly because he didn't want to draw attention to his night wear. The flannel pajamas he'd gone to bed with the previous eve had suffered a transformation overnight.

Do you like it?

The nice penguins had become red-eyed, fanged versions with curled horns. Very vicious looking.

Exactly.

"Lucifer wants to come with us," she told Remy.

At his name, Lucifer beamed. How happy the fire demon would be to know they would go to the beach together and fight, side by side.

"What do you mean he wants to come?" Remy grimaced. "His coming wasn't part of the plan."

"I know," she muttered. "It took me by surprise, especially given how he reacted on Dante's ride."

"Excuse me," Lucifer said, ignoring his demonic penguins as he scrambled out of the bed finally.

Gaia cringed. "Would you stop it with the manners already?"

"What plan are you talking about?" He peered at Gaia then Remy, who both did their best to look innocent. And failed.

What did they hide?

Wait for it. Wait for it. Come on. You know the answer.

His jaw dropped. "You totally expected me to stay behind and avoid the fight."

Gaia shrugged. "Yes, I did. And I still do. You don't like icky things like blood and guts. Why would you want to drop wedding planning for a down-and-dirty, beachside brawl?"

The horned duckie in his head practically bounced. *Wanna go. Wanna go. Wannnnnnna goooooo.*

It shouldn't have sounded appealing. It shouldn't have pricked his pride. But it did.

"I'm going." He puffed out his chest. Gaia wasn't the only one who could play heroic.

"No, you're not. It's too dangerous for you. But don't worry, sugar cakes." She patted Lucifer's cheeks. "Once I'm done handing Ursula her ass, I'll come back and fix you."

Fix us?

He should totally put her over his knee for that remark. Wait. That thought hadn't come from his other side. Stay in control. Starting with his fiancée. "I am coming, and you can't stop me!"

Actually, she could. She blew some kind of powder in his face that rendered him somewhat lethargic but not completely impotent. It took a dozen of his minions to tether him to the bed with the chains she claimed to have, "*Found in the garbage and thought I'd bring them back up.*"

Straining at his tethers, he found it hard to not

let irritation color his tone.

"Let me go, Gaia."

"What, no mushy nickname?" She smirked. "Maybe even if I can't get your heart back, there's hope for you yet. In the meantime, I am going to save you and save Hell. The glory shall be mine. See you later, *baby*." She crooned the word and winked.

She did not just call us an infant.

On the mortal side, it was a term of endearment.

She knows I hate that word. I. Am. A. Man. I deserve manly names.

Except Gaia didn't currently see Lucifer as a man. *She thinks I'm weak*. She wanted to keep him safe and save Hell.

They all did.

A part of him struggled to convince himself that this just showed their depth of caring, but deep down, real deep, he knew the real reason they tied him down.

Because I am too great.

You are?

They know that in battle I will outshine them all. With my mighty sword, I will smite the most enemies. If I was on the battlefield, I would be the hero. The one soaked in the most blood and glory.

Maybe. He'd never know for sure since Lucifer kind of found himself shackled to a bed.

Are you really going to let chains stop us?

Uh, yeah.

Wrong answer. Have you forgotten who we are? Who I am?

Lucifer. Former inhabitant of Heaven until he'd left that boring plane to his brother. He was the devil, the Lord of all Sins.

What about the Lord who was taking a sabbatical to plan for a wedding while, at the same time, hoping to turn over a new leaf?

Bang. Bang.

Lucifer caught himself before the third head smack against the headboard.

Ouch. Stop that.

Stuff a pair of dirty panties in it and repeat after me.

"What if I don't want to?" Ignore the fact that Lucifer spoke aloud to the voice in his head, the voice that shouldn't exist.

Are you really going to test me? You won't like it.

The voice proved right again. He didn't. His mouth moved, and not by his volition. It spoke, in a dark and terrible voice. *"I. Am. Lucifer. Lord of Hell. Eater of souls. The king of retribution. Chains mean nothing to me."*

Snap.

#strongerthanilook

Chapter Fifteen

@GaiaLuc4ever: I'm coming for you, Ursula. #gonnawhoopass #gogogreenpower

ON THE BEACH BY the summerhouse Lucifer maintained—where many a vacation Hell memory was forged—Gaia stood, stave in hand, stray hairs floating on a sea breeze.

I'm here. Ready to meet the hag who dared screw with her. And Gaia wasn't here alone.

The dark legion spread across the beach and the bluffs, an evil force gathered for one thing. One person.

Turning her back to the rolling waves, she faced the legion. She knew from centuries of watching Lucifer at work that motivation and a strong leader were necessary for all battles.

"Why are we here?" she shouted.

"Because you said so!" they yelled.

Good start. "We are here," she stated as she thumped her staff in the sand, "because the sea hag Ursula has stolen something of our Lord. And we are going to get it back!"

Clang. Clang. Clang. Weapons on shields and rock and anything thumpable, including shorter comrades, the noise filled the air as they chanted, "Get it back. Get it back." The treble of their song shook the very foundation beneath their feet.

To keep their blood fired, she went on with her impromptu speech. "The forces against us will be mighty."

As if that would dampen their enthusiasm. "Yay!"

"This battle might prove deadly."

"Bring it!"

She eyed them, these eager imps and demons and other creatures gathered. She had only one more thing to say to them. The trigger words. "Be relentless. Be victorious."

"We shall show no mercy!" Remy shouted. "For we are the legion of darkness."

"Hooyah."

"We shall crush them," the ogre-ish contingent yelled.

"Stomp them," boomed the giants.

"Make them wish they were the load their mother spat out." Remy's evocative addition.

"Slice them into bite-sized chunks for a beach bake," yelled a ferryman from a bobbing flatboat as he shook his oar aloft. While the cloak hid his face, Gaia recognized Adexio's voice.

Everyone had come to give her a hand against Ursula. Gaia wasn't planning to leave this beach without Lucifer's heart—and that sea hag's head.

She felt that moment when the future of Hell sat at the tip of an axis. They all did.

"Monster!" someone yelled.

Gaia whirled to see a purple eye stalk bob from the waves alongside Adexio's craft.

"Hold your fire," she hollered, recognizing SWEETS.

Adexios huddled with his pet a moment before

announcing, "Ursula's army approaches. Remember to use the bombs on the kraken."

Any more words he might have spoken got drowned in the sudden boil of ocean water, not the heated boil from a flame, but that from hundreds of creatures thrashing upwards from its depths.

Aerial predators also swooped from the sky. Strange monsters not of this world, nor this dimension.

Ursula had proven busy building her army, drawing from the dimension that, until recently, had held her prisoner.

She might have lots of monsters to throw at us, but that's all right because I've got a hungry army. "Legion! Attack."

With a cry of excitement, the soldiers and minions surged over the dunes and through the choppy waves on the beach. Some demons soared overhead, strapped onto the backs of drakes, the smaller cousins of the dragons.

The Vikings chanted as they stroked their longboats farther from shore, heading for the waving limbs of the rising kraken.

"Row row row our boat through the choppy sea
Until we find a big fat fish
And stab it 'til it bleeds."

Catchy tune, but not one she had time to hum as creatures slopped onto the beach and humped across wet sand. Others skittered on spindly legs, clacking pincers. A few, like the Undines, the deadly progeny of Hell's mermaids, walked on two legs and swung coral swords.

The legion met the threats.

It wasn't just from land that they fought. Nor

from the sky. Neptune himself also joined the fracas, jabbing at the bobbing beasts with his mighty trident, while his son, Tristan, arced and flashed through the waves, a pair of scimitars in hand. No surprise, Muriel rode a chariot drawn by hellphins. Her consort, Auric, swooped on shadow wings at any stray tentacles that came too close.

Stray glances were all she could spare as she found herself engaged with the enemy. They swarmed the space around her. Every swipe of Gaia's machete, every jab with the sharp points on her fingers into something jellylike that burst, had to count. As she whirled and sliced something new, she caught a different glimpse of the battle.

There went Marigold clicking her fingers and turning rampaging brackish crabs into pink ones with bow-wrapped pinchers.

Thrust. Jab. Gurgle. Spin.

A group of Undines went waddling past on webbed feet chased by Katie who wore nothing but a bikini and a smile. "Woooooooo," she screamed, her voice fading in tenor as she streaked past.

Duck. Kick. Ouch as someone yanked at her braids. Crunch as her head thrust back and broke something.

Spin around and she noted Nefertiti standing atop the bluff, arms upraised, body nude, and yet covered by hands, dozens of them as her harem fed her magic. She lobbed electrical darts at thrashing tentacles splitting the waves.

Drop to a kneeling position. Gut the bloated hellfish on two mutant legs. Take a deep breath and narrow her gaze as a tremor of wrongness hit the force all around her.

She's here… The unmistakable stench of her presence was a discordant note she couldn't ignore.

A note she would silence.

Standing, Gaia tossed her one remaining machete to the side and drew the stave strapped down her spine. She shook it until it grew, its knobby grain stretching. The staff was formed of the wood from the oldest tree in her garden, given as a gift for her to fight the forces against nature. A thing of beauty that extended to whatever length she required, the ends sharpening into points.

"Oh, Ursula. Over here," she sang as the sea hag slithered onto the beach, the tentacles beneath the skirt of her dress peeking from under the hem.

"If it isn't Lucifer's whore. Oh wait. That was last week. Way I hear it someone isn't going around flashing his dick anymore. Not even to his own fiancée."

"Hate to break it to you, but my sex life with Lucifer is just fine. Better than fine. Orgasmic. According to him, I was finger-licking good, unlike someone else we both know. I hear someone has an odor problem." Gaia smirked. Pricking someone's pride was the surest and quickest method to get them to lose their composure.

Red suffused Ursula's features, and her eyes flashed stormy blue waves with white-crested peaks. "Keep your manwhore. Not all of us wanted to spread our legs for the devil."

"Afraid you'd lose the stick in your ass?" Gaia laughed as rage made the hag tremble.

"I am going to take great pleasure in stuffing that mouth of yours with sand." Clapping her hands together, Ursula then held them out, palms raised.

From the rolling waves at her back leaped a pair of swordfish, their snouts pointed and sharp.

Even though Gaia didn't physically touch the creatures, she could sense the wrongness about them. The perversion tainted the very air around her. "What have you done?" she asked.

"I did what I had to in order to survive and entertain myself. I created. Some of the friends I made only needed little nudges to become what I needed; others," she intoned grasping the handle-shaped tails, "needed a little more work."

"That kind of gross manipulation of things with free will is wrong." Gaia rarely imposed her will upon the world. The world just kind of reacted to her emotions and thoughts. It also gave her whatever she wanted, and in turn, she cared for the world.

But Ursula thought only to use and abuse. "Free will is only for those strong enough to have it. Everyone else is fair game."

"If you mastered the dimension you were in, then why return?" she asked. The hag certainly didn't seem happy here.

"Can't a girl come home to visit?"

"I think you've overextended your stay."

"Less talk!" yelled Valaska as she dashed past Gaia, covered in blood. "More fight."

A good reminder. While Gaia blabbed with a villain, the legion faced incredible deadly odds. Remember what Muriel had said. Delaying the fight did nothing but delay the inevitable. Ursula had to die.

"Give me back what you took," Gaia growled, advancing on the blood-soaked sand, stave held in a ready position.

"Make me."

With those taunting words, it was on!

While Ursula jabbed with her modified fish sticks, Gaia twirled her staff, using it to block jabs and thrusts. She landed a hard tap on Ursula.

The hag grunted and threw herself back.

Striking a pose, leg extended, sending a scurrying purple crab flying, Gaia regarded Ursula, the hint of a smirk hovering on her lips. "Are you done already? Gonna take your toys home to your other dimension?" She hoped not. There were still some anger issues requiring resolving.

"We are just getting started, you hippy whore."

"Hippy?" Gaia danced to the side. "I'll have you know I haven't looked like a long-haired flower child since the eighteen hundreds." If she didn't count the times she played the part of naïve virgin in the garden and Lucifer played himself, the snake... But that was less about peace and love than it was about raunchy, screaming sex.

Gaia ducked as something shot from a sucker on a waggling tentacle. Splat. Whatever it hit behind her cried out once and then fell to the ground with a thump.

"Loogie tossing, really? Are we children in the dawn of time still?" she taunted.

"Does this seem childish to you?" Ursula spun, her tentacles whirling like a dervish on the sand, her arms extended, sharp blades slicing the air.

Ducking under the onslaught, Gaia managed a slice across Ursula's mermaid dress. She really wished she hadn't, given the fabric dropped and everyone got to see what was really under that skirt.

Writhing, moist tentacles, mauve-ish gray in color. And the smell…

"Stinks like dead fish."

"That's not what Lucifer said when he tried it."

"Liar. He never touched you."

"He might have been drunk, and the cave dark, but he most certainly did."

Oh. Gross.

Possessed of a berserker rage, Gaia flung herself into the fight. She knocked the swordfish from Ursula's hand. A moment later, she missed her timing on the handspring and paid for it as the rotation of the tentacles flung the stave from Gaia's grip.

It didn't stop the fight. Onwards they grappled, fighting hand-to-tentacle for the right to live.

Only one of us is going to be able to claim victory. A grim determination possessed Gaia. *I will win.* Defeat was not an option. More than half of winning was the right attitude.

The rest was cheating, Lucifer had whispered to her more than once in the past.

Gaia yanked the dagger from her thigh, and while she wouldn't risk tossing it, she could use it to slash.

Ursula hissed as a line in her flesh welled with blood. "Tricky garden weed. Would you just give up and die?"

"Get stuffed and roasted over a fire." As Gaia spoke, she kicked the stave now within reach into the air. Her hand shot out and grasped it.

Armed again, she twirled her staff, banging it off Ursula's arms and straying tentacles. The onslaught proved quick and tricky. The hag fell back, her blubber-butt hitting the sand.

Gaia did not relent. She pressed the sharpened end of her stave against the squishy flesh of Ursula's third boob, all that stood between Ursula and a permanent death.

"Give me back Lucifer's heart," she demanded.

Despite the direness of her position, a smug smile pulled Ursula's lips. "I can't."

"What do you mean you can't?" Gaia leaned forward, knowing the end of her staff punctured the outer layer of skin but not caring. "I know you took it. Now give it back, or I will end your miserable existence." Mercy was for those who deserved it.

"You still don't get it, do you? Did all those pesticides fry what smarts you had? I can't give it back to you because he already has it. The heart beating in Lucifer's chest is his own."

"That's his heart?" The words slipped out on a faint breath filled with incredulity. "Impossible. No. You're lying."

"No lie and you know it." Ursula's grin twisted into a sneer.

"It can't be Lucifer's. The heart in his chest is polite and caring. Lucifer's heart is—"

"Not as black as you'd think. The demon had it removed so long ago it had a chance to recover. A little purifying in Elyon's antiseptic pool in Heaven and—"

"You've been to Heaven?"

"Indeed I have. A touch too bland for my tastes, but it served its purpose. It turned the devil into a pussy. No more Mr. Badass who thinks it's okay to lock me away in another cold and dark dimension just because I tried to have him killed a few times. And just think, soon you'll be married to that puny imitation for eternity. The reign of the so-called Dark Lord is over."

The knowledge hit Gaia with gale wind force.

She mentally reeled, and Ursula took advantage.

This close, Ursula didn't miss with the trident formed of seawater that came spearing forth.

Despite Gaia's armor, the tines sank through, their touch icy cold. The pain proved sudden, and she couldn't help but scream and then scream again as it pushed deeper. Gaia, on the brink of possible death, sent a plea out to the one person she always called to when she needed help. The one person who always came—even if he complained about it. "Luc!"

#ineedahero

Chapter Sixteen

@GaiaLuc4ever: I'm baaaaaaack. Bow. Grovel. And beg for forgiveness. #lucifer4ever #gonnawhoopsomeass #hammertime

THE CHAOS OF BATTLE reigned all around him. Lucifer didn't cringe though. He did not wipe the specks of blood that spattered his new outfit. Black jeans, black nylon shirt, toe flip-flops, oh and sunglasses, which he realized might have been overkill.

This outfit needs a cape.

Capes got caught. Better not to wear one. At least he'd changed. He'd almost run to battle in his mutant pajamas.

Strutting through the fighting masses, Lucifer spent a moment seething about how this had come to pass. He'd lost his mind to the light side and all because of a heart. His defective heart.

Nothing wrong with caring.

See that cage, the one you kept me in? Why don't you pay it a visit?

Or how about I put you back in there?

The problem with a mental battle, especially one where you represented both sides, it was a lot harder to cheat.

His fight with his goody-two-shoes half felt like a bitch slap fest. But that all changed at the strident cry of his name.

"Luc!" Gaia called for him, but he couldn't see her amidst the fighting bodies.

Where is she? He vaulted onto the back of something chitinous and with his new height could see the battle-beach clearly.

Saw his sweet wench clutching at her midsection. Reeling backwards, his earth goddess fell. The quivering weapon, thrusting upright from her body, collapsed in a splash of liquid, but it wasn't enough to wash away all the bright green blood as it flowed from the grievous wounds puncturing her body.

She's hurt.

More than hurt. She was about to die. Ursula rose above her, a new watery trident held aloft, triumph in her gaze.

She's going to kill my wench!

That evil fucking hag thought she was going to kill his woman? Like hell.

Rage exploded in him, a molten heat that coursed through his limbs and burned all futile resistance away.

Whatever shadow of good that still clung to him shed under his glorious return. He jumped from the crustacean, the force flattening it. He stood taller as he drew in the power he could harness around him.

I'm back. And he was fucking pissed.

Lucifer strode forth. With each step, his bearing drew more rigid, his eyes burned more fiercely, and a snap of his fingers was all it took to have a fabulous cape streaming from his back.

The legion parted before him, sensing his greatness. As for the enemy in his path, he swept a hand and bowled them from his shores. They had no place on his land.

Ursula caught sight of him and paused before pulling her arm back, preparing to plunge her trident.

With everyone's attention on him—where it belonged—Lucifer bellowed, "Drop that fucking oversized fork, you fishy-smelling hag, before I spear you on it and roast you over the coals of Hell!" By the time he finished yelling, smoke poured from his ears, and his entire body was wreathed in a red glow.

"You won't hurt me. It would be a sin," said Ursula with a smirk.

"I know. And I'm way behind on my quota." He snapped his fingers, and chains shot up from the shore of the Darkling Sea and wrapped around her shape.

Idiots always forgot Hell was his realm. *Mine.* And while he might allow them to play in it for sport, ultimately, he ruled it.

When the hag would have spoken, he slashed a finger in the air and stole the air from her lungs and around her. He stomped, and with each step, the ground trembled. All of Hell trembled.

"I allowed your return to this realm because I thought perhaps you'd learned to behave, or at least not be so fucking stupid." He stopped before Ursula, noting the fear in her eyes. Liking it.

He tilted her chin, and a cruel smirk twisted his lips. "I could have perhaps respected your need for vengeance against me, but you should have never, ever touched my wench."

Only I touch her.

Most times Lucifer believed in a long, drawn-out tortuous retribution. Usually.

Today, he took a page from Muriel's book.

He beheaded Ursula and, with a flick of his fingers to his legion, ordered them to, "Chop her to pieces and scatter her remains on as many planes as you can reach."

A great leader didn't bother to see if they obeyed. They would or face his wrath. Besides, he'd already wasted too much time.

He dropped to his knees by his wench, worried by her waxy pallor. With every second, she inched away from him. So he did the only thing he could. He stopped time.

#who_s_bad

Chapter Seventeen

@GaiaLuc4ever: Those must have been some good 'shrooms. #lucisback #seeingbirdies

TWEET. TWEET. Chirp. Twirl.

The little birdies flew drunkenly inside her eyelids, bright red and blue, flapping about in all their cartoon glory, her subconscious mocking Gaia's most girly swoon.

I think I'm allowed a bit of a moment, considering I've been stabbed with a fork! The holes in her stomach stung. Not to mention leached her strength. Nothing like the poison of another dimension to bring a girl down.

To which her drunken birds, with no regard at all, uttered a shrill, *TWEET!* Translation: Suck it up.

Apparently, her subconscious birdies enjoyed channeling Lucifer's creed.

Still, they weren't as annoying—and welcome—as the voice cajoling her. "Come on, wench. Open those damned eyes. Stop being such a lazy ass. Napping in the middle of battle. Or is this your way of breaking your word? If you think you're going to get out of the wedding by dying, then you've got another thing coming. I will chase you down in the afterlife. A deal is a deal. I am not letting you escape my grubby clutches that easily." Then more gruffly. "Don't you dare die on me."

Sounded as if she was dead already because she

could swear that exasperated tone belonged to Luc. Her Luc. The way he should be. Annoyed and bugging her.

Perhaps she'd suffered a concussion when she swooned. How else to explain her hopeful auditory hallucination?

"Have you forgotten I know when you're faking? It doesn't work in bed, and it won't work now."

As if she ever had to fake it. Lucifer would never leave her hanging. Even he wasn't that selfish.

Did the voice truly belong to him? Fear made her want to keep feigning sleep just in case she dreamed.

Don't be a coward.

She pried open a single eye and almost blinked it shut as she saw his dashing face, set in a dark scowl, hovering over hers.

Lucifer never was a man to give her personal space. She rather liked that, despite his claims they should remain aloof in public, lest she ruin his street cred. He often broke his own rule, staking his claim on her in subtle, at least to him, ways.

His face lowered so that his iris hovered only a few inches above hers. In its depths she could see the always-burning fires of Hell. "She lives," he announced. "Not that I'm happy or anything about it one way or another. Really couldn't give a damn."

At that blasé announcement, she almost burst into tears of joy. She refrained because, much like a nervous hellcolt, the slightest sign of tears might send Luc bolting. She stuck to finding out if it truly was him. "What do you think of world peace?"

"Wish they'd get on with it because all this

sinning cuts into my golf game."

"Low fat diets?"

"Discriminatory to delicious carbs and calories."

"What's your favorite dessert?" The true question as to who controlled Luc's body right now.

"Everyone knows it's cinnamon apple pie. Your pie." He licked his lips, and she could almost see the memory of the last time he'd licked her reflected in his gaze.

"It really is you. You're back."

Lowering his head, he brushed his lips over hers and let the wicked tip of his forked tongue tease the seam of her lips. "Damned straight I'm me. The Lord of Hell is back. Past time too."

Wrapping an arm around his neck, she clung to him, noting that he held back, careful to not press against her wound. "But how?" she murmured against his neck, inhaling his familiar scent, a heady blend of sin and brimstone that, until now, she'd not even realized he lacked.

"How she asks? Because of you. I should say no thanks to you. You know, if you wanted to shake me up, you didn't have to almost die. What were you thinking letting that hag distract you like that? Epic fail on your warrior skills there, wench."

"So sorry I disappointed," she retorted. "I'd just gotten some distressing news."

"Nothing is worth your life."

She ran her hand down his cheek, loving the burn of his heated skin. "I don't know if I agree with that. Not that I would care what happens to you, of course," she lied.

He noted her blatant fib and smiled. "Exactly.

Just like I certainly didn't go after Ursula to save you or anything. It wouldn't be dignified for a man of my position. Not to mention, getting involved in the rescue-a-damsel business would set a bad precedent." His expression soured in annoyance. "You know how I hate being gallant. It ruins my image."

"So did wearing that apricot-colored ascot last week," she said through a watery giggle of relief.

A moue of distaste twisted his lips. "Don't remind me. I plan to perform a major campaign to restore my bad name. Can you believe the nerve of myself, dressing and acting like such fucking ninny? I should slap myself. And then set fire to my wardrobe. I am still utterly traumatized by the fact I got rid of my awesome collection of demonic alligator underwear."

While Lucifer prattled on about the various things that he'd have to rectify—from the fact that he'd sung soprano, and not because someone kicked him in the balls, to the emasculating incident where he helped an elderly imp cross the road—Gaia used that halted moment in the space-time continuum to pull herself together. Literally.

Lucifer stopped time—*for me*—and, in the doing, stopped the flow of her sap. Or blood. The name depended on which scientist was playing with a sample at the time. She did so love screwing with them.

The fork wounds, on their own, weren't life threatening, not anymore, but they sure did smart. She winced as flesh knitted together, winced even harder in fake pain just to have Luc's fingers stay wrapped tight around hers as he prattled.

Caught in this moment in time, a moment she wished she could set in amber, she allowed herself to enjoy the relief and pleasure of having Luc back.

He eventually caught on to her ruse and stopped talking about himself to address her. "Are you done delaying the inevitable?"

No. She'd like to delay the inevitable a little longer. "And what is the inevitable?"

"You, in my lap, bouncing up and down and squealing your joy at my return."

Sounded like fun. "I don't know if I'd call it joy," she hedged with a smile. "I mean, the other you did have impeccable manners."

"How horrifying. He also put the seat back down after using the bathroom."

"I know," she said with a chuckle. "The staff couldn't wait to tell me, figuring you had a girlfriend on the side." She'd fed them to her roses for being tattletales. "I still can't believe it's you."

All healed up now—or at least enough until she could enjoy a good root in her garden—she flung her arms around Luc's neck and yanked him down to her. In true Lucifer fashion, he collapsed atop her, squishing her with his weight.

She loved it, although not for too long because a girl did have to breathe. After a moment, she shoved at him, and with a sigh and forbearing, "If I must," Lucifer put himself on his forearms. "Have you quite finished polluting my sand with your bodily fluids? If I am not allowed to give you real, organic pearls to wear in public, then you may not dirty my beach."

"Forgive me, Your Highness, for bleeding to death."

"Obviously not to death. For had you died, the whole world would have tasted my wrath." For a moment, his eyes darkened, a dark endless abyss of night and cold, the cold of the dead in their grave. "If you're quite done being a drama queen, get your ass off my beach and into this lap."

Lucifer never did anything so simple as sit in the sand. With a flick of his wrist, he reshaped his part of the beach. Drawing her against him, he held her as the land around them gave him a throne.

"King of the Beach? Really?" she said as she stood on the sandy dais.

Seating himself, he reached for her and dragged her onto his lap. "I was actually going to go with The Dude King."

"But you can't surf."

"Yet!" he said. "I know a minion who could give me lessons."

"And I know the perfect girl for him," she said, now familiar with this matchmaking game he liked to play. Why toy with mortal lives when demon and other Hell realm ones proved so much more interesting?

"I can't believe you're back and that you're you. Ursula said that prissy heart in your body was yours all along. But she must have been lying. Did you finally rip it from your chest?" She placed her hands on his upper body, noting the hardness of his muscles under the black silk he wore. A steady beat met her touch.

He noted her surprised look. "My heart is still in there and still trying it's best to drag me back over to the good-two-shoes side."

"You mean you might turn back?" She couldn't help a hint of panic.

"No, I think I'm safe now. I figure a few more days of corruption and my heart will turn black and shove that polite bastard out."

Seated in his lap, Gaia gazed at him, so glad to see the familiar scowl, the naughty mischief, and the hard lines in his face, the kind that screamed, "Yeah, I'm an asshole, but you love me despite it."

And she did. Just like he loved her. Enough that a threat to her life had snapped him back to himself.

I wonder if I should be flattered that I bring out the asshole in him.

"So when are you planning to remove your heart again?" she asked.

But before he could reply, time snapped back.

Gaia let the commotion of the battle's aftermath wash over her. With her head cradled against Luc's chest, she had no desire to move. And oddly enough, he didn't make her. He actually allowed a public display of cuddling. And not a single snowflake to be seen.

Lucifer sat upon his throne of sand and presided over the beach, a beach they'd held their ground on and taken by force.

Fist pump for the legion. They won the day.

Clean up had already begun, with Remy and a few other minions holding open interdimensional portals to dump the corpses in. Funerals were for mortals.

It didn't take long to get rid of the unwanted waste. The choicer sea specimens were hauled off and prepped for dinner.

Recycling was a way of life in the pit. Resources proved too scarce to waste, and there were a lot of hungry legionnaires. And Vikings.

Never forget the Vikings…

Hungry ones were never a good thing.

A few very large and lapping waves took care of the remaining filth on the beach, Neptune taking great delight in brandishing his mighty trident as he lorded it over the water.

Until a hellgull pooped on his head.

Judging by the smile tugging at Lucifer's lips, not an accident.

With each bellowed order, the chest under her cheek rose and fell, the commanding tone a pleasant rumble. She basked in the arrogant superiority and ribald attitude Luc displayed. She soaked it in, a woman parched for the man she loved. A Dark Lord many had missed.

The pleasure in his return showed in the grumbles—"Taskmaster!"

"Look at him lording over us in his chair."

"The boss is back, and there's gonna be some trouble. Yay."

My lover is back.

Mmmm. Lover. There was something else she'd missed during his absence. Having him. In her. On her. Anything with her.

She squirmed on his lap, and he noticed. Luc *always* noticed.

His lips brushed her ear, hot with promise. "Soon, wench. Very. Very. Soon."

Why reply when she could wiggle against the hard bulge under her bottom?

He growled against her lobe before nipping it. "Such a naughty wench tempting me to ditch my duty."

"I am so very naughty," she whispered back. "Want to punish me?"

"Yes. Just you wait until later."

Later? She pouted. He nipped her lower lip totally inviting what came next. Gaia straddled him and totally showed his mouth who was boss until Muriel yelled, "Ew. My eyes. You've fucking blinded me."

Her daughter, the one in a committed five-way relationship, was such a prude.

Because of Muriel and a beach full of other spectators, all Gaia could manage were nibbles and gropes. She didn't tease alone. Lucifer also taunted, letting his finger dematerialize enough to go through her skirt so he could stroke the skin of her thigh without anyone noticing.

I noticed. Her pussy noticed. Luc noticed and rumbled naughty things in her ear, always with the word later.

Later arrived after a few more hours because, of course, such a grand victory over the enemy deserved a celebration. As Hell's version of daytime fled and bled into darkness, they feasted by the light of giant bonfires, the flames of which, fed by the fire demon contingent, leaped into the air in a primitive dance.

The smell of roasted crustacean had more than one mouth watering, and taste buds tingled at the smoky flavor, enhanced by the butter drizzled on it.

Delicious. Especially when hand-fed by Luc. Each succulent morsel he fed her left the tip of his finger in her mouth. She sucked it, each tug of her lips pulsing a spark of light in his eyes.

She fed him the same way, unabashedly groaning as he sucked her finger, all too easily imagining that same caress on another part of her.

By the time Lucifer whispered in her ear,

"Ready for bed?" she was more than aroused. She was ready to rip the clothes from him and ride him until the cows came home. Which, considering they had no cows, would take a long, long time.

Without announcement, Luc stood with her in his arms. They escaped the party still in full swing through a portal Luc called with a snap of his fingers. In a moment, they'd gone from the noise and revelry of the beach to the silence of the hall outside his room.

He set Gaia on her feet, his hands on her waist. Finally alone and with a bed only steps away.

As her fingers reached to grab the handle to open the door, she found herself propelled against it. Luc's body molded to hers, every strong, demonic inch.

About time. She leaned her head against the door and took pleasure in looking upon his face set in a sultry smile.

"Well hello there," she said, her voice husky. "I see someone is happy."

"I will lie vehemently if asked, but it's nice to be home."

"I wasn't talking about that." She reached around his solid body to cup his ass. She jerked him closer, reveling in the feel of his erection pressing against her, a solid presence even with the layers separating them.

"I wouldn't call this happy," Luc replied with a grind of his hip. "Painful. Frustrating. In dire need of care."

"We can't have that," she murmured, brushing her lips against his, not letting him capture them yet loving the tease.

A chuckle and his eyes twinkled with mischief. "You want me to get busy again? From my recollection, you owe me one."

"One excellent blowjob coming up." Usually, she would playfully argue about it, a version of foreplay for them. But she was so happy to have Luc back.

Before she could divest him of his pants and drop to her knees, he grabbed her hands and held them tight. "Oh no you don't, wench. Do you know what tomorrow is?" he asked.

"Call in sick so we can fornicate day?" Lucifer declared those quite often.

"Nope."

"Bring a minion to work?"

"They already all work for me."

"Are we having another bacon day? Because, you know, we've already had three this past month."

"It will be four if I have my way. And you are trying my patience, wench, with your deliberate obtuseness. What is tomorrow?"

Surely he wasn't talking about, "Our wedding?"

"It is indeed our wedding. In less than twenty-four mortal hours, you will belong to me."

She wrinkled her nose. "Are you still planning to go through with it? I'll admit I kind of figured, now that you were back, you'd find an excuse to cancel it."

"Never. Tomorrow, I will claim you in the eyes of everyone."

The ominous sound of it sent a shiver through her. "You say the hottest things," she purred. She wound herself tighter to him, only to find herself set away.

"Behave, wench. We are not wed yet."

Blink. "Are you still rejecting me?"

His thumb rubbed across her lower lip. "Never. But I am going to follow one tradition. No sex for you, especially not tonight. Abstinence, dear wench, will make your pussy fonder."

"I hate you."

The smile he shot her was a blend of lust and affection that smacked her emotions and wobbled her knees.

"I know."

#ishouldhaveusedthatstake

Chapter Eighteen

@GaiaLuc4ever: Thinking of running to the ninth ring. #someoneobject #whatwasithinking

COLD FEET WERE expected, especially from Lucifer. After all, the Lord of Sin getting wed, how perverse and unnatural. He complained loudly to all who would listen.

"I'm supposed to be breaking up marriages, not getting into one."

Lucifer stomped about with grand theatrics. He, Hi, Ho, hum, where did everyone hide his rum?

A proper diva, he had a fight with the wedding planner. And won. There would be rubber ducks, not fish, in the artificial pond.

All kinds of things he did and said that morning, but as the hours passed, he did nothing to stop the big day. Although he did make quite a few modifications.

During his temporary insanity, he'd done a fair number of things he didn't approve of. Such as ordering a tuxedo, a white one, with a pink cummerbund, vest, and kerchief.

Fuck no.

A stroke of his hand down the tuxedo took care of color. Black was the only fitting color for a day like today. He also adjusted its fit so that the cut would flatter his current physique. Time enough after the wedding to return to his older, more distinguished appearance.

The shirt he kept snowy white, but only because it highlighted the bowtie he pulled out of hiding. He'd had it specially designed the day after he proposed to Gaia. Then hidden it because she'd threatened to burn anything but a traditional neckpiece.

As if he would ever be completely boring like that. The ghoulish skulls on the tie appealed to him, and he smiled as he adjusted it around his neck.

"No duckies?" Muriel, with a lack of manners he applauded, entered his room without knocking.

"I'm wearing ducks, just not where anyone can see them."

"I should have known." Her nose wrinkled as she minced toward him in chunky shoes and a flouncy pink monstrosity with big bows and a giant corsage. "I wish you'd turned back into good daddy in time to change these bridesmaids gowns to something less hideous." Muriel pinched the fabric with distaste.

It made his next words so utterly delicious. "But I did change the dresses. My alter ego had you wearing something form fitting and elegant. Blech. Couldn't have that. How else are we to get outrageous images and mocking tweets? I want all of Hell to talk about this day." Not to mention, he didn't need the wedding party outshining his grandeur.

"You are the worst daddy ever!" she huffed. Her arms flung around him and dragged him close for a hug. "Love you, Daddy. Glad you're you again."

He patted her back. "I'm a little fond of you as well. A little," he repeated when she hugged him tighter.

"I don't suppose I can use that fondness against you and have you call off this travesty?"

"I am marrying your mother. Today. So suck it up, princess."

"Argh. I hate you both," Muriel screeched as she stomped off.

A bratty, ungrateful wretch. What a perfect gift for him on his wedding day. Lucifer smiled. Protest as Muriel might, he could still see the happiness within her, as well as the reason for her bitchiness. He wondered if her harem knew Muriel now ate for two?

Probably not, given Muriel thought herself barren. *I guess Gaia didn't tell our daughter she fixed her.* Subterfuge and secrets. How wonderfully evil.

Exiting his room, he ran into Ysabel, looking fetching in a medieval flame-colored gown. Alongside her, Remy looked utterly too dashing in his dress uniform.

I am the star of the day.

What of the bride? his other half, more like an eighth now, interjected.

The bride belonged to him. And she should have eyes only for him as well.

Lucifer snapped his fingers and changed the color and fit of Remy's uniform, and all of his other close guard, to something a little more bile green and loose.

While Remy couldn't prevent a grimace at the change, he didn't object. "The guests have arrived and are gathered in the grand ballroom."

"All of them?" he asked with a quirked brow.

"Your son, Chris, and your brother, Elyon, declined to attend."

Ah yes, his supposed son, who'd renounced his

father and his antichrist heritage. He kind of expected that. The boy had issues.

As for Elyon…a stab at his heart made him thump his chest. It did not bother him at all that Elyon wasn't coming. The goody-two-shoes would have probably sniffed sanctimoniously and ruined a night of debauchery.

"Are the groomsmen assembled?"

An unnecessary question because he strode into the ballroom as he asked. Spanning a few football fields in length, it looked utterly opulent and greenly lush.

It seemed his plans to turn the place into a jungle had worked. Even better, his nice side had approved of his choice made before the fiasco with his heart and had not done anything to ruin it, other than changing the horned duckie ice sculpture to a swan.

As if a swan could inspire terror. That took only a snap of the fingers to correct.

As he took long strides towards the altar—upon which many a sacrifice had bled its last—he noted all the chairs, thousands of them, filled with folk. Deities he'd known growing up. Others who shared a parentage. Minions who cowered under his command. Couples he'd forced into relationships. Results of amorous encounters.

It's called friends and family. They're here because they care about you.

He almost gagged.

He also felt all warm and fuzzy inside.

"Someone fetch me a drink!" He held out his hand, and a passing imp slapped something with crazy-high alcoholic content in it.

Refreshing.

As Lucifer reached the head of the aisle, Neptune, his best man, leaned forward and said, "Dude, run. There's still time. Don't do it."

Poor Neptune. The seagod with a hag for an ex-wife.

"There comes a time in every demon's life when he has to stop avoiding a fate worse than death and get married. That time is now."

Now as in this very moment. He could tell because the music abruptly stopped and a hush fell over the grand ballroom.

As overlord of Hell, he should have been above the petty temptation to watch his bride walk down the aisle. He did her a favor by marrying. Yet, that didn't stop his gaze from straying, and he stopped breathing.

At the far end of the aisle stood his wench. Her gossamer-thin green gown flowed from her, as did her hair. She'd grown it long for the ceremony, Rapunzel long. Flowers weaved its length.

Upon her taking the first step, the music started, a hauntingly beautiful creation unlike anything ever heard. It accompanied her graceful float past the guests, the train of her gown held aloft by little pixies with jewel-colored wings.

A soft spring breeze fluttered through the room, lifting tendrils of her hair, whispering about with promises of new beginnings.

Other grooms might find themselves faint as their future approached on mincing steps. Other grooms might run when faced with a future with one woman.

Lucifer broke tradition and walked toward his bride. Why should she have to come to him alone? This was a journey they should take together.

As he reached her, he halted and held out his hand. There was no need for words.

With a smile she only ever had for him, she wrapped her fingers around his, and to more haunting strains, they made their way to the altar of pledging.

No official presided over their nuptials. There was no higher power great enough to do the job.

They did it themselves.

Facing each other, her eyes a bright grass green, they spoke their vows.

Hers, a poetic promise, "On this day, I join myself to thee, forsaking all others. Binding my fate to yours, no matter what the future brings. Always and forever."

As for Lucifer, he had no need of flowery speech. He got right to the point. "Ditto. Now does anyone object?"

A hand rose in the crowd, that of the elven queen of the forgotten realm. "I object. The earth mother should not bind herself to evil."

Without even turning her head, Gaia pointed her finger at the elven queen, shooting forth a bright beam of light. The protesting guest dissolved into glittery dust motes. "Anyone else have a problem?" she asked.

Pure silence.

"By the power vested in me, because I am awesome, I declare this woman mine. Which means"—Lucifer glared at the crowd—"covet, hurt, or even think about her wrong, and you will die."

The declaration was met with whistles and cheers, even a standing ovation as everyone rose to their feet. Frenzied clapping accompanied a chant of, "Kiss the bride. Kiss the bride."

Hell yeah. Yanking her hard against his chest, Lucifer took a moment to reward Gaia with a leering smile. Then he dipped her low before claiming her mouth in a kiss to put all other kisses to shame.

In that moment, he laid his claim to her. Sealed her with his mark. And she claimed him right back, the passion in her embrace enough to make even this old demon's knees weak.

When they finally parted for breath, the cheers almost brought down the centuries-old ceiling. As it was, a few stone blocks flattened some unlucky guests, but that didn't put a damper on the festivities.

The band struck up a song, and his impish staff milled among the guests, bringing out the tables for dinner, rearranging seats, setting out more food and snacks.

But Lucifer wasn't staying for the reception. His blue balls were too painful for that.

Tossing his new bride over his shoulder, he made his way across the vast ballroom, scowling at the repeated well-wishes.

Gaia, on the other hand, took great delight in their rude departure. She waved and giggled at the more ribald suggestions.

As if Lucifer needed any pointers when it came to what he should do in the bedroom. He wrote the book. Made the movie. Invented all the moves.

Everyone else now merely imitated.

And palely at that.

Once they hit the hall, Lucifer quickened his pace.

"In a hurry?" teased Gaia.

"Don't mock me, wench. I have needs."

"Then why are you taking so long?" she

growled. With a snap of her fingers, they went from hall to bedroom.

Whereupon she flipped off his shoulder and slammed him against the wall.

"Ooh, getting rough." He leered. "I like it."

"Get naked," she growled. "But leave the tie on."

"Kinky too. Even better." It took him but a snap of his fingers to divest himself of his garments. Why waste time undressing when he could watch Gaia slipping out of her wedding dress? It fell in a silken pool of fabric at her feet, leaving her naked.

Gloriously naked. And attacking him.

His very naked wife threw herself at him, her lithe limbs wrapping around his hips while her lips latched onto his with a voracious hunger.

He fisted her hair in his hands, just as eager as her. Maybe more so. Arousal controlled his every thought. He was a male after all.

And as the man in this marriage, he rolled them until her back pressed against the wall. He freed one hand and used it to delve between her thighs. His finger slid across the moist flesh of her sex.

Wet. Hot. The more he touched, the more Gaia moaned.

No demon could resist. He thrust a finger into her. Then another. Her hips undulated against them, sucking at them tight.

As he finger fucked her, he parted her lips that he might invade her mouth with his tongue. He wanted to leave no part of her untouched.

With his thumb, he rubbed her swollen button. He thrust faster into her sex, feeling her mounting excitement in the way her hips rolled with his movements and her breath turned into pants.

He could have brought her to the edge of bliss, then and there, with his fingers. But he was a selfish devil. He wanted her to come on his cock.

The tip of him pressed against her sex, thick and hard. He might have taken a moment to tease them both, yet her limbs cinched tightly around him, drawing him close, driving him in.

The width of his shaft stretched her. Filled her tight. As he thrust into her velvety sheath, he kissed her, kissed the lips that belonged to him.

Kiss the chin he owned.

Kissed the ears he claimed.

And when they came, she took whatever he had that passed for a soul.

Their climax brought them to a place out of time and body, a place where their spirits could twine, forever one.

Given his man card probably wondered if he'd need another intervention, he didn't say anything too stupid or sappy, just held Gaia close, but that was acceptable, given they were both naked.

The wall, however, proved uncomfortable. A quick levitation was all it took to land them in bed, a much softer spot.

As their sweaty limbs cooled, her head rested on his chest, where the steady thump of his heart caused her to lift her head and regard him with a frown. "So when are you going to conduct the ritual to rip it out?" she asked.

Such a bloodthirsty request, and on their wedding night. She knew how to spoil him. "I don't know if I'm going to do that. I'm thinking maybe I'll just leave it where it is."

The shock of his words had her scrambling to an upright position so she could gape at him. "Keep it? Why would you do that? You know wearing it in your body makes you vulnerable."

"It does, and yet…" He pressed his hand against the skin just under her ribcage. "I see you also have yours close by once again. Why did you do it?" He'd noticed, despite all the layers of spells she'd laid upon her heart.

Head drooped, she replied. "I got it back during that fiasco with Lilith. She came too close to finding it. I figured it was better off with me. And then"—she fingered the fabric of the comforter they lay on—"I didn't want to put it back. I didn't realize how much I wasn't feeling until it was a part of me again."

"Bingo. Give my wench a prize. Too late, you already got one. Me!"

"Wait a second." Her gaze rose to meet his as her brow knit into a frown. "I just admitted I kept it so I could feel. What's your excuse?"

He flipped her onto her back and crawled over her body until he hovered over her. His eyes glowed with a reddish fire. "I might be a bad fucking bastard."

"The baddest."

"I might be the king of sin."

"None can compare," she said with a smile.

"But I find myself quite liking this abnormal affection I have for you, an affection that is enhanced by my heart."

"I thought it was black."

"It is. Mostly." His lips twisted. "But a teeny-tiny part, the smallest part, is fond of you. Very fond. Why I might even say it loves you."

"It does?"

"Very much. But"—he leaned down until they touched nose to nose—"tell anyone and I will deny it. And probably kill anyone who hears it."

"Keep it a secret. Gotcha. No problem. Wouldn't want to ruin your reputation after all." She smirked.

"Glad you understand."

"But since we're alone, and no one else is around, could you say it again? To me. Please."

His brow knit. "Manners? In the bedroom?"

She laughed. "What was I thinking?" She grabbed him by the ears and yanked him close. "Tell me you love me, you big fucking bastard, now, or else."

A slow, sensual grin curved his lips. "That's more like my wench. I." He rubbed his nose against hers. "Love." The word whispered across her lips. "You." He claimed her mouth, but only for a moment before flipping her onto her back on the bed and rolling away. "Before I forget, I have something for you." He stood, stretching his youthful frame, preening under her admiring glance.

He then reached within and gave her his present. She totally screamed.

#blew_her_mind

Chapter Nineteen

@GaiaLuc4ever: When you think you know someone and they do something unexpected, just for you. #mindblown

"WHAT THE HELL ARE you doing?" She knelt on the bed and held his heart, not a black organ like he'd claimed. Not even gross and bloody like she expected.

It pulsed warmly in her hands. A living. Beating. Part of Luc.

"I am giving you my heart."

"You do realize that expression isn't supposed to be taken literally."

Hands planted on his hips, Lucifer frowned at her. "Wench, stop vexing me. I am giving you my heart because it is my wedding gift to you."

Expression incredulous, she stared at him. "You would give me your heart. The thing that makes you mortal?"

"I trust you with my life. My affection"—he couldn't help a curl of his lip—"and my cock. Which, as you know, is technically more important than that defective thing."

At his repugnance, she couldn't help a smile. For all his brashness, Luc cared. Cared too much, but as Lord of Sin, he couldn't let it show, except with her.

His wife.

After shoving it back in his body until she

could think of a safe place for it, she then showed him what his love meant to her.

Their passion leveled a few mountains. Woke a few dormant volcanoes. And world peace was declared for all of eighteen seconds. A record.

And while peace couldn't last forever, they could, a forever that could last a long, long time considering their lifespan, but she could handle it, knowing the biggest, baddest demon loved her.

And together they would rule both Hell and Earth.

#together #forever

Epilogue

@GaiaLuc4ever: Do not disturb. #Mine #Sorryaboutthetsunami #NoIamnot

AS THEY LAY CURLED in a pile of sweaty limbs, all belonging to living bodies, their own to be exact, Lucifer couldn't help but feel…happy.

Stupid side effect from the heart he'd given Gaia that needed a good corrupting. He'd gone a long way in starting with his ravishment of Gaia all night long, but it would take some time before his heart achieved its previous level of darkness.

Although perhaps he'd keep a smidgen of it free of sin, just a tiny spot, mind. Nothing like throwing his new wife and family off balance with the occasional sincere compliment or sudden gesture of affection.

He did, after all, care for them, kind of, in a roundabout sort of way that totally made him want to scrub himself in a bath of sulphuric salts.

Damned emotions.

"What are you thinking?" Gaia asked as she tickled her fingers up his chest.

"I'm thinking that, now that we're married, we should totally torture the minions I've matched with couples dinners."

She giggled. "Sounds like fun."

"Speaking of fun, where's my present?"

"What present?"

"Don't toy with me, wench. You tethered me with a ball and chain. Caused thousands of hopeful women to declare themselves spinsters for life. And I let you have a drawer in my dresser for your stuff. That deserves a present."

"About that…" She rolled onto her side and propped her head on her hand. "I kind of struggled with what to get you. I mean, you've got just about everything a demon can have."

"I do." No point in being modest. If he wanted it, he owned it. Or cheated at cards to get it.

"So, I thought to myself, what can I give Lucifer that is kind of unique? That would be something only he would want."

"Sounds promising. What is it?" A custom-crafted Lucifer-mobile? Another dimension to rule? A reign of darkness over the mortal realm?

Gaia grasped his hand and placed it over her rounded abdomen.

It took him one sharp, indrawn breath to realize what she showed. A spark of life.

A son.

In that moment, his mind flashed as hundreds of visions slammed him with a precognition he'd not experienced since the last time he'd impregnated Gaia.

I'll be damned. He might be the eater of souls, but according to what he saw, his son would be the devourer of worlds.

Best present ever.

Fist pump.

#fetchmeacigar

THE END

Made in the USA
San Bernardino, CA
01 July 2016